He Must Have Pulled The Craziest Stunt Of His Entire Life By Marrying That Woman.

Jeremiah had *never* responded so strongly to anyone in his life, nor had anyone ever responded that way toward him. But he had to let Bridget have her freedom, chalk last night up to a fantasy and get on with his life.

Yeah. He'd tell her she was right, that what had happened was insane. Besides, *his* feelings weren't the only ones he had to consider. He had—

"Jeremiah?"

He was so deep in thought that he had no idea his privacy was being invaded until he heard the husky female voice.

He swung around and stared at the woman who was now his wife and knew with a certainty born of old that he could never willingly let her go.

Dear Reader,

Can you believe that for the next three months we'll be celebrating the publication of the 1000th Silhouette Desire? That's quite a milestone! The festivities begin this month with six books by some of your longtime favorites and exciting new names in romance.

We'll continue into next month, May, with the actual publication of Book #1000—by Diana Palmer—and then we'll keep the fun going into June. There's just so much going on that I can't put it all into one letter. You'll just have to keep reading!

This month we have an absolutely terrific lineup, beginning with *Saddle Up*, a MAN OF THE MONTH by Mary Lynn Baxter. There's also *The Groom, I Presume?*— the latest in Annette Broadrick's DAUGHTERS OF TEXAS miniseries. *Father of the Brat* launches the new FROM HERE TO PATERNITY miniseries by Elizabeth Bevarly, and *Forgotten Vows* by Modean Moon is the first of three books about what happens on THE WEDDING NIGHT. Lass Small brings us her very own delightful sense of humor in *A Stranger in Texas*. And our DEBUT AUTHOR this month is Anne Eames with *Two Weddings and a Bride*.

And next month, as promised, **Book #1000, a MAN OF THE MONTH**, *Man of Ice* by Diana Palmer!

Lucia Macro,
Senior Editor

Please address questions and book requests to:
Silhouette Reader Service
U.S.: 3010 Walden Ave., P.O. Box 1325, Buffalo, NY 14269
Canadian: P.O. Box 609, Fort Erie, Ont. L2A 5X3

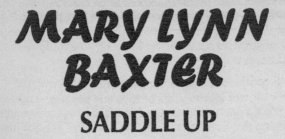

MARY LYNN BAXTER

SADDLE UP

SILHOUETTE *Desire*
Published by Silhouette Books
America's Publisher of Contemporary Romance

To my aunt, Bess Hinson,
for all the years of love and support.

 SILHOUETTE BOOKS

ISBN 0-373-05991-4

SADDLE UP

Copyright © 1996 by Mary Lynn Baxter

This edition published by arrangement with Harlequin Books S.A.

® and TM are trademarks of Harlequin Books S.A., used under
license. Trademarks indicated with ® are registered in the United States
Patent and Trademark Office, the Canadian Trade Marks Office and in
other countries.

Printed in U.S.A.

MARY LYNN BAXTER

sold hundreds of romances before she ever wrote one. The D&B Bookstore, right on the main drag in Lufkin, Texas, is her home as well as the store she owns and manages. She and her husband, Leonard, garden in their spare time. Around five o'clock every evening they can be found picking butter beans on their small farm just outside of town.

Dear Reader,

Saddle Up was such a fun book to write, as marriages of convenience are one of *my* favorite reads. I hope they're one of yours, too. The story involves a rancher in Utah, Jeremiah Davis, who is a widower and lonely. Yet he's leery of making another commitment—until he enters an auction for charity and is won by a stranger in town, Bridget Martin.

Their attraction is hot and instantaneous. And through circumstances seemingly beyond their control, they end up marrying the day they meet, making the secrets each harbors as lethal as their attraction.

I'm honored to be counted among the Silhouette Desire family. Writing for Desire is like anticipating a Friday night date; it's thrilling, titillating and highly entertaining.

Saddle Up is a part of the Desire **Celebration 1000,** which makes this book extraspecial to me. I hope you, as a reader, will find it just as special.

Mary Lynn Baxter

Prologue

—

Jeremiah Davis had once been a proud man—proud of his land, his cattle and his wife. Now, as he rode across an open pasture looking at the fence that would need mending next week, he thought about something his father had told him as a child—pride goeth before a fall.

And fall he had, as far from upright as the rotting miles of fence posts stretching into the horizon. First, he'd made a bad investment—one that had cost him his financial cushion, leaving him on the edge of disaster. Then, a bad calf crop had devastated any profits for this year. Finally, his wife had been taken from him.

He was a lonely man now, bereft of everything that had once meant so much to him. Pride. Again he thought about the word.

The Davis ranch was in southwest Utah. The closest town, Pennington, was comprised of a general mercantile and one filling station with a cold water fountain. Once daily, a train flew through town, causing all the otherwise indolent hounds to howl and show a sudden burst of energy before settling back into the Utah dust.

Maybe he should call it quits. To hell with ranching. It was all his father had ever done, and what had it gotten him? Jeremiah looked into the horizon toward Hurricane, a town where he could get a *real* job. But did he truly want a real job? How could he survive in the eight-to-five world of asphalt, suits, choking collars and "Let's do lunch"?

The ranch house loomed ahead, a native rock structure that had once glistened with the attention of his mate, someone who'd shared his love for this land. Now, the house reflected his emotions, almost as ramshackle in appearance as his inner turmoil.

To hell with this, he thought. He could wallow in misery from now on and nothing would be accomplished . . . but if he didn't eat something soon, the Davis graveyard would have yet another inhabitant.

Once inside, he tossed his hat on a nearby chair and strode to the kitchen, popping a skillet onto the range. A couple of eggs cracked into the pan might have worked if he'd added a little bacon drippings, but what did he know? He and Margaret had had an understanding. She didn't try to run the ranch, and he didn't try to run the house. Instead, the eggs stuck, turned black, filled the room with smoke and set two dogs to howling.

Disgusted, he dumped both eggs and the skillet in the garbage and opened his last bag of pork cracklings. Dammit, something had to change.

The phone interrupted his tantrum, and he answered it with a mouthful of cracklings.

"Hey, Jeremiah. What's up?"

"Same garbage, different day, Nelson."

"You sound funny."

"It's my lunch—straight out of the bag."

"Sounds like you're chewing on dried locusts. Listen, if you need a meal, come on over. Sharon—"

"Thanks, but no thanks. Last time I showed up, you had some heifer from Nevada all lined up for me."

"Speaking of heifers, that's what this call's all about."

"Forget it. I'm not interested in another woman. I've told you that already. *No* just has one syllable, so what's your problem with understanding it?"

"You need to listen, Davis. What I'm about to ask you is in the best interest of the whole community. Hell, maybe even all of southern Utah."

Jeremiah rolled his eyes, knowing Johnny Nelson. His ranching friend was a good man, but persistent as a rash. He would have to hear him out just to get rid of him.

"Okay, shoot."

"We're going to have an auction, my friend."

"I already lost my shirt at one auction this year. Why in hell should I want to go to another one?"

"No, you'll *love* this one."

"All right," Jeremiah said in a resigned voice. "Go on. I'm listening...."

One

"**B**ridget!" Tiffany cried. "Check out what's on TV!"

Bridget Martin ran to Tiffany's living room carrying a bowl of dip and a bag of chips. "What is it?"

"Look for yourself. I've never heard of anything like this before."

A WNN talk show host was interviewing two uncomfortable looking men who were sitting on a couch.

"Now *that's* a hunk of manhood!" Tiffany pointed to the one on the left.

"What's all this about?"

"Shh. Listen."

Bridget wasn't keen on the two men being interviewed. Neither caught her fancy. Both were okay as far as looks went, but then, she wasn't such a good judge of that right now. Men were *not* at the top of her priority list.

"Did you hear that?" Tiffany was asking.

"No, what did he say?"

"You're not listening!"

Bridget did as she was told and found the gist of the conversation not only incredible, but insane. The men were from a remote ranching community in southwestern Utah, close to the Nevada state line, where, apparently, there were more men than women.

As a result, these men were advertising the fact that they intended to hold a community auction and put themselves and some of their friends on the block, hoping that women would come from all over the United States and bid on them.

"But aren't there *any* local women?" the host asked. "I mean, why can't you—"

Tiffany's hunk spoke up. "The nearest single women our age are a long way off. When I take a lady home after a date, I'm lucky to be back at the ranch by daylight, and there's still a day's work ahead. We're mostly farmers and ranchers...and we can't afford to lose time chasing all over southern Utah and Nevada."

The camera focused in on the host, who was all smiles. "There you have it, ladies. You heard it first on WNN. If there are any of you who need a man, here's your chance."

He turned his attention to the men on the couch. "So, exactly where is this auction taking place?"

"Pennington, Utah," the hunk replied, then gave the date and time.

"And do you men keep the money that's bid on you?"

The other man, a half hunk, shook his head. "No, sir. All proceeds from this auction go to a shelter for battered women, not that we have many of those. All we're asking for is the chance to meet some eligible—

and hopefully attractive—ladies who wouldn't mind ranch life in Utah.''

Bridget groaned, then added, ''Sure thing, buddy. I'm real anxious to spend my life barefoot and pregnant in southern Utah! In between kids, I could rope steers and brand calves. Maybe take a few quilting lessons. Yee hah!''

Tiffany turned to Bridget, her face animated. ''This is a hoot. Let's go!''

Bridget rolled her large brown eyes, even as her smile broadened. The word ''dramatic'' fit Tiffany Russell to a tee. But then, that didn't seem so odd when she remembered that Tiffany's ambition in life had been to be an actress, only that hadn't panned out. Instead she'd had to settle for working in one of Houston's largest and most prestigious department stores as a buyer for women's clothing.

Too bad becoming an actress hadn't become a reality, Bridget thought, because with Tiffany's long blond hair, gray eyes and sharp wit, she would have been a killer on stage. But it wasn't to be.

''God, Tiff, what would make anyone want to go bid on some sodbuster, anyway?''

''I don't know...I guess I'm just bored. My life's headed straight down the toilet.'' Tiffany gestured dramatically as if to better illustrate her point.

Bridget laughed outright, only to suddenly turn sober. ''Believe me, I know how unhappy you are.'' She paused. ''If it's any consolation, my life's headed in the same direction...but I'm still not grabbing the next plane to Pennington, Utah!''

''Do you suppose planes even land there?''

''Who knows? From the way those men made it sound, you probably have to fly to Salt Lake City, then work your way down by pack mule. What do I know about Utah?''

"About as much as I do. Still, your life's not in the toilet. That's a bunch of baloney, and you know it." Tiffany's lips curved downward. "Oh, just forget I said anything. It's just that I'm down. I hate my job so much."

"Well, at least you have one," Bridget countered on a more sober note.

Tiffany's eyebrows perked up. "I'll trade places with you anytime. Heck fire, you're a big-time Houston lawyer with brains and looks."

"And no job, remember?"

Tiffany made another gesture. "Not for long. Every firm in this town will soon be knocking on your door."

"Wrong, Tiff. The very second word got out that I filed a sexual harassment suit against Mason Wainwright, the you-know-what hit the proverbial fan. From then on, my name was mud. Job or no job, as long as I remain in Houston, it'll stay that way."

"All the more reason to take a mule to Utah!"

Bridget's voice took on its best courtroom tone. "Miss Russell, there are games of chance and games of *fat* chance. My going to Utah comes under the latter category, even if there's no future left here for me."

"That's not true, and you know it. Your old man's one of the best attorneys in Houston, and he's got clout! Why, he can open doors for you that would be cemented shut for the normal person. All the other firms are afraid of him!"

"Even if he was willing, I wouldn't let him." A pained expression dulled Bridget's features. "Right now, I'm not his fair-haired child. He and Mother are both... upset."

Tiffany's lips formed a semblance of a smile. "Why don't you say furious and be done with it?"

Bridget's answering smile was equally lukewarm. "Okay, they're furious."

"See? Don't you feel better having gotten that off your chest?"

Both women were seated on the couch in Tiffany's apartment, which looked more like an art deco studio than a typical Houston dwelling. Tiffany had rented the upstairs in an older home in the refurbished Heights area and furnished it with upscale junk, or at least, that was Tiffany's way of describing it. Although Bridget would never even have looked at this place, much less lived here, it fit her friend's personality perfectly.

Now, after reaching for an oversize pillow near her, she tossed it at Tiffany. "No. As a matter a fact, I don't feel a bit better. I'd rather tell them to their faces what I feel."

"Then why don't you?"

"They'd both have heart attacks on the spot."

"So?" Tiffany grinned.

"You're bad to the bone, girl," Bridget said, but found herself grinning, as well.

"I'd rather call it truthful."

"Okay, so my parents went ballistic when I brought that civil suit, but they're still my parents."

Tiffany frowned. "Look, I didn't mean—"

"I know," Bridget interrupted, her tone distant. "First off, they've never learned how to loosen up. And second, they expect me to be just like them."

"Which you're not and never will be."

"Sometimes I think I must've been adopted. As uptight as they are, I can't imagine them conceiving *me!*"

"Sorry, but you look too much like your mother. And, I might add, she's *still* a knockout."

"She'd thank you for the compliment." Bridget paused again. "Right now, my parents are pretty far down on my list."

"That's too bad, but I understand. Hey, you want some coffee?"

Bridget shook her head and plunged a potato chip into the clam dip. "No, but if you have any tea made, I'll have a glass."

"I'll make some," Tiffany said, getting to her feet and heading for the kitchen. "Instant only takes a minute."

Bridget watched her leave, then reached for another pillow and hugged it against her chest. She wondered if her friend really did understand, having come from a household of five other siblings and parents who let their kids do their own thing.

Even though Bridget couldn't identify with that kind of upbringing, she envied it. She had been born with a silver spoon in her mouth. Added to that was the curse of being an only child. She bore the brunt of everything right and everything wrong, according to her parents' rules.

Bridget hugged the pillow closer, her thoughts still stuck on her parents, who at the moment were more an aggravation than an asset. If only they had been more supportive of her decision to file that suit, things might have been different. Hell, if they had been even a little supportive, she wouldn't be in the predicament she was in now.

Unfortunately, they had been anything but supportive. In fact, they had been outraged and demanded that she withdraw the suit minutes after she'd returned from the courthouse.

"How dare you do something like that without consulting me first?" Allen Martin had bellowed.

"Why, Dad? You weren't the one Wainwright tried to maul! Besides, I'm grown and responsible for my own actions."

"Well, you sure couldn't prove that by me."

"Your father's right, honey," Anita Martin had chimed in. "I can't believe you'd smear a good man's name."

"Didn't either of you hear what I told you? Dammit, Wainwright—"

Her father had cut her off, his voice cold. "Not another word, young lady, especially using that kind of language. Mason Wainwright is a longtime friend and excellent attorney. You know we all go to church together—or you *would* know if you'd attend more often. He's a deacon, for heaven's sake! Hardly the type to come on to you like a man of the world!"

Bridget's laugh was bitter. "Oh, he's a man of the world, all right—with Russian hands and Roman fingers!"

Allen bristled. Anita gasped.

Bridget wanted to scream, unable to believe this was happening. How could they take that vile man's word over hers? She shouldn't have been surprised, though. Despite her father's retirement, he kept in touch with everything that was going on in the legal field through his "of counsel" status, and his expert opinion was still sought after by a host of attorneys. However, in Bridget's heart, nothing excused his siding with a man she knew to be an oversexed hypocrite, deacon or not.

"Look, it's obvious you think I'm making a mountain out of a molehill, and that's okay. You're entitled to your opinion. But I'm not going to back off."

Much to her dismay, she *did* have to eat her words and back off.

"I bet I know what you've been thinking about," Tiffany said in a disapproving tone, waltzing into the room and setting Bridget's iced tea on the coffee table. "Your parents, right?"

Bridget sighed, then rubbed the back of her neck, registering her exhaustion. "You're right."

"So are you going to listen to them?"

"As in dismissing my suit?"

"Yep."

"I already have."

"Honestly, Bridget, when are you going to let them stop running your life?"

"I didn't do it for them, Tiff. The other attorney in the office, the one who was supposed to corroborate my story, since she'd been a victim herself, clammed up. She refused to testify, and there went my case. Without her, it's a swearing match."

"Mmm, sounds like old Wainwright put the screws to her."

"I suspect he threatened to blackball her just like he did me, only she's divorced with two kids to consider."

"So what *are* you going to do?"

Bridget shrugged her slender shoulders. "Start pounding the pavement, I guess. I still have a burning ambition to become every bit as good a litigator as my dad or better, then open my own practice. Working for these large firms isn't my cup of tea. Unfortunately, that's the only way you can get the experience it takes to make it on your own."

"Only now you're ostracized."

"That's a mild word. You'd think I had leprosy or something."

"It's really that bad, huh?"

"Yes, it is." Gloom was mirrored in Bridget's face. "I can always go to Dallas, or maybe San Antonio—if I can get at least one good recommendation from the firm."

"I wouldn't count on it."

"I'm not."

"So what does Hamilton think about all this?" Tiffany raised her hand. "Don't answer that. Let me guess. He's as furious as your parents."

"Righto."

"Jerk."

In spite of her friend's sarcastic tone, Bridget's lips twitched in good humor. She just couldn't get mad at her friend. "I guess it's safe to say that you don't like my fiancé-to-be."

Tiffany snorted. "Fiancé, hell. You have no intention of marrying Hamilton Price. You never have. If anything, he's too much like your old man, more so, actually. Hamilton wears his underwear so tight, it's a wonder he can breathe."

"Please, don't start on Hamilton, okay? Besides, we're a long way from walking down the aisle. We're not even engaged."

"Good . . . cuz I gotta tell you straight, friend, you and Hamilton have nothing in common. *Nada*. El zippo!"

"I know," Bridget said, sighing.

"At least there's one bright point in all our misery."

"And just what is that?" Bridget asked.

"It's not what, it's where." Tiffany pointed at the screen. "There!"

"You've *got* to be kidding."

"Hell, no, I'm not kidding. I'm more serious than I've ever been in my life."

Bridget harrumphed. "Well, as far as I'm concerned, you're on another planet. Circling Jupiter would be my guess."

"Hey, come on, where's your sense of adventure?"

"Where it ought to be, in the toilet, along with my career."

"That's exactly what I'm saying. That's why we both need a change of scenery."

"But you're working, Tiff. You didn't get fired."

"Yeah, but I have oodles of vacation time I haven't taken."

"I almost believe you're serious."

"You're damn straight I'm serious."

"But...but why?" Bridget sputtered.

"Because it's something different. It's a hell of a good way to look at some great bodies—" Tiffany paused and giggled. "And who knows, I might even find one I'd like to spend the rest of my life with."

Bridget stared at her friend in amazement. "I don't know whether you've gone completely off Jupiter or you're just plain old horny."

"I expect it's a bit of both." Tiffany wrinkled her nose. "So what do you say, want to go with me?"

"Not on your life."

"Why not? You need to lighten up. You take life far too seriously. Anyway, what can it hurt?"

"Nothing, except that it's a waste of valuable time, time I don't have."

"Oh, come on," Tiffany pleaded. "Do it for me."

"I love you, Tiff, and I'd do almost anything for you, only not this. There's nothing you can say or do that would convince me to go with you to that god-forsaken place."

"Wanna bet?"

"Yeah, I'll bet. How much?"

"Fifty bucks," Tiffany said.

Bridget grinned, scrambled off the couch and headed for the door.

"Where are you going? You haven't even finished your tea."

"I'm leaving before some of whatever you're suffering from rubs off on me."

"Chicken." Tiffany wasn't satisfied in just saying the word. She had to follow it up with wing-flapping and a few *buck-buck-bacaws*.

Bridget shrugged. "Call me anything you like, but the answer is still no."

Tiffany repeated the noise.

Ignoring her, Bridget added, "And while we're at it, you might as well fork over that fifty bucks ahead of time. There's no way I'd even consider such a cocka-mamy thing."

Two

Bridget had to admit this part of the country was beautiful. She lifted her head, her gaze tracking the tall pecans and cottonwood trees as they ballooned upward. Around her were mountains the color of red bricks, flanked by fertile valleys covered with buffalo grass.

Still, Bridget couldn't believe she was here at the auction in the backwater town of Pennington, Utah. Worse, she was parked in the front row of the Pennington Civic Pavilion, gawking like the other women packed onto the plastic folding chairs. At least, Bridget told herself, she wasn't gawking for the same reason. For one thing, the auction hadn't begun yet, though offstage the men she guessed were participants stood laughing and talking. The other women, including Tiffany, were watching them with blatant curiosity.

Bridget refused to lower herself to do more than glance in their direction, mortified that somehow Tiffany had managed to get her way after all.

"Well?"

Tiffany's whisper jolted Bridget to the moment at hand. "Well, what?" she asked in a vexed tone.

Tiffany laughed. "You know what."

"You want your money."

Tiffany rubbed two fingers together, her grin widening. "I'll take it any time you're ready to give it to me."

"I'm surprised you're just now asking." Bridget's tone was churlish at best.

Tiffany's laughter deepened. "Hell, I wasn't sure you'd actually go through with it."

"What did you think I was going to do? Jump out of that damn puddle jumper they call a plane?"

"No, but once we got here, you could've refused to go any farther."

"If I had half a brain, I would've turned around and taken the next *Spirit of St. Louis* back to Texas."

"Aw, and miss out on all this fun? Come on, pay up, then let your hair down, for heaven's sake. We'll enjoy the auction, get a load of eye candy—" Tiffany nudged Bridget's shoulder "—eat some barbecue, then head to the motel."

"And then go home, right?"

"Only after we see a little of the country," Tiffany said. "I've never been this far west, and I aim to take advantage of it. Besides, once the auction's over, you should be able to get that pained expression off your face and have a good time. You look like you just saw Wainwright again!"

Bridget threw up her hands, but she couldn't stop the smile that spread across her face. "You're impossible."

"That's why you love me so much. Now, about that fifty bucks..."

"Damn you, Tiff!"

Tiffany merely laughed as Bridget slapped bills into her friend's outstretched hand. She watched as Tiffany made a kissing sound before stuffing the money into her purse.

"Go to hell," Bridget whispered.

"Thanks, I will, with a new purse hanging on my shoulder. This fifty smackers will help pay for it." She paused. "It's going to be all right, I promise. You'll have a good time."

"Sure I will, Tiff. I'll probably cherish this moment forever...like I would having all my teeth pulled," Bridget mumbled under her breath, turning away from Tiffany's mischievous eyes.

Tiffany nudged her again, harder. "Hey, take a gander at that fellow with the black hair and mustache. He could do anything he wanted in my bed."

"Behave yourself! You act like you haven't had any in a long time."

"If you're referring to nooky," Tiffany whispered, "I haven't. Remember, you're the one with the man."

Only she hadn't had any from him in a long time, Bridget thought, her mind turning to Hamilton and the hissy fit he'd thrown when she told him that Tiffany was trying to talk her into going away with her for a few days. Even now, she could see Hamilton in her mind's eye. Tall and always impeccably dressed, which only heightened his gym-toned body to perfection, he was handsome in a stodgy sort of way. A successful stockbroker, his best asset was perfect white teeth, which he used to charm his clients. But on that particular day, the smile had turned into a grim frown.

"Why would you do a thing like that?" he'd asked with unusual bluntness. "You know how I feel about *her*."

Bridget saw red, as she did so often of late when she was in his company. "You don't have to like her. She's my friend."

"I still think you could do better. After all—"

"Save it, Hamilton. I don't care what you think about Tiffany, or any of my other friends, for that matter."

He had looked at her for a long time, that frown still in place. "What's happened to you?"

Bridget played innocent. "What does that mean?"

"Oh, I think you know. Ever since you went off on that crazy tangent with that civil suit, then quit your job, you're not the same person. I don't know you anymore."

"Maybe you never did." Her tone was flat, with a tinge of sadness.

"So what are you saying, Bridget?"

"Nothing, for the moment, except that I think we should cool our relationship for a while."

"If you ask me, that's already happening. You haven't let me near you in so long I've forgotten what it's like."

"Sorry, but I'm going through a bad time, and without any help from you or my family."

He flushed. "Well, that's because we don't agree with what you're doing."

"Well, *thank you* for all the support, Hamilton! That lets me know exactly how you feel about me."

"That's not so. You're—"

Disgusted, she cut him off in mid-sentence. "Forget it. I don't want to hear any more."

That conversation had taken place yesterday, and now she was wondering why she hadn't listened to

Hamilton, at least as far as this trip with Tiffany was concerned.

Heaven help her, but she felt she indeed had taken complete leave of her senses. Why had she done this? she asked herself again, even as a band struck up an unfamiliar country song that sounded like someone whining through his nose from inside an oil drum.

So what if her nerves had been on edge? So what if she'd received a lot of bad press and publicity from her lawsuit? So what if her parents were treating her like the family pariah? Though certainly disconcerting and depressing, it nonetheless didn't warrant this erratic and out-of-character behavior.

She was a grown woman, thirty-one years old. She'd had lots of rejections in her life, mainly from her parents, who treated her more as an object to look at, to be proud of, rather than a flesh and blood person to be touched and loved. Even so, she'd never given in to self-pity or done anything stupid. Until now.

This situation was intolerable in every sense of the word. Surrounded by the aroma of barbecued meat, sitting among other women dressed in jeans and boots and listening to a horrible band loud enough to burst an eardrum was not her normal idea of entertainment. The women next to her and Tiffany were laughing and giggling as though they'd never seen a man in their lives. Their behavior was especially embarrassing in the circumstances, for Bridget couldn't ignore the TV cameras and reporters planted around the stage and among the crowd.

"Are you ready?"

Bridget shook herself mentally and faced Tiffany. "For what?"

"God, will you get with the program? The auctioneer just stepped up on the stage."

"How will I ever contain myself?" Bridget asked, adding as much sarcasm as she could muster.

"I know what you were thinking, so just stop it, will you? You're here now, so you might as well make the best of it. Please, will you try to loosen up and enjoy yourself?"

Bridget couldn't ignore the pleading in Tiffany's voice, nor did she want to. She knew she was acting like a nitwit and hated herself for it. But at the same time, she was out of her element here, and was miserable. She should be in Houston, dressed in a three-piece suit and working with other attorneys in a courtroom. Instead, she was dressed in tight-fitting jeans, a Western shirt and boots that were killing her feet. She sat on an uncomfortable plastic chair, facing a pavilion that was little more than an oversize gazebo, watching a man approach the podium with a gavel in his hand.

Thank God, the late spring weather was cooperating. She didn't think she'd ever seen a more perfect day. Warm, but not too warm. And the sun bouncing off the huge red rocks was so brilliant that it was almost blinding. It was beautiful here. The land was breathtaking, and Bridget imagined there were seldom many humans to block the view.

"Okay, I'll give it a rest," she responded at last. "But if you ever try to talk me into anything like this again, I'll cut you up into tiny little pieces."

Tiffany's laughter was drowned out by the loud voice of the auctioneer.

"Ladies and what few gents there are here—" The man standing behind the podium with a gavel in his hand was tall and burly. It was apparent he reveled in the laughter that the word "gents" brought from the ladies.

His moment in the sun, Bridget thought, then scolded herself for her satirical attitude.

"I'd like to welcome you to the first event of this kind anywhere in the United States of America."

"That's for sure," Bridget muttered under her breath, for which she received an elbow to her arm from Tiffany.

"Will you shut up and behave yourself?" Tiffany whispered. "But more than that, watch!" She threw Bridget a grin that was tinged with disgust. "Who knows, you might fall in lust with the first cowboy who saunters onto the stage."

"Maybe in another lifetime, if I'm reincarnated as an idiot," Bridget said, then focused her attention on the speaker.

"Have we got a treat in store for you ladies today," he was saying. "Then, after the auction is over, we'll all have a rousing good time eating, drinking and dancing." A huge grin narrowed the auctioneer's eyes until they were almost invisible. "Can't beat that, now, can we?"

"No!" the crowd of women yelled at him, followed by a round of laughter.

Looking over her shoulder, Bridget gasped. She'd had no idea so many women were in attendance. Since they had arrived early at Tiffany's insistence and plopped down in the front row, again at Tiffany's insistence, she'd had no idea that the crowd had grown to such an extent. But then, she shouldn't have been surprised. As the auctioneer had said, this event was one of a kind. Where did all these horny women come from? Didn't they have any sense of decency? My God, you would think they were running loose at Chippendale's!

And Bridget was right in the middle of it, in the middle of this bunch of women with whom she had

nothing in common and never would. She mustn't
forget about the roving TV cameras, either. She had
to avoid them at all costs. Her parents had no idea
where she was or what she was up to. If they saw her
on national TV—well, that thought didn't even bear
thinking about. Allen Martin would descend on her
with the holy wrath of Jehovah! She ducked her head.

"And now, ladies . . . for our first stud, Mr. Ken
Jefferson."

Another round of whoops and hollers filled the air.
Bridget wanted to put her hands to her ears, but she
knew if she did, Tiffany would box those ears.

"Wow! Take a gander at what just strolled onto the
stage."

At Tiffany's words, Bridget jerked her head up and
perused the man who was walking as if he had a corn-
cob up his backside. She didn't know what Tiff saw in
him. He did nothing for her, sexually or otherwise.
Apparently she was in the minority, though, for the
women in the audience went wild, whistling and calling out amounts that made her head spin.

"Holy cow!" Tiffany said. "Can you believe this?"

"No, I can't." Bridget's voice was low and flat.

Tiffany chuckled. "I swear, if I had the money and
didn't have a job, I'd bet just for the heck of it."

"If you think for one minute that just because *I*
don't have a job, I'd—"

"Hey, I was just teasing. Of course, you can't bid,
and you wouldn't if you could. Daddy might ground
you or something."

"You're right, I wouldn't. But I'm not worried
about Daddy," Bridget lied.

"Still, it would be fun."

"No way. You might actually *win!*" Bridget said in
a churlish tone. "Anyway, what happens when they
bid and win one of these men?"

Tiffany shrugged. "Beats the hell out of me. I figure they'll strike up an acquaintance and go from there."

"Which is where?"

"To the altar, then the mattress," Tiffany said, giggling. "But not necessarily in that order."

"That's disgusting!"

"Only to you, friend. After all, that's the purpose of this auction. These men need to find mates, someone who'll work side by side with them in this part of the country."

"Well, I wish them all the luck in the world."

"Ken, here, my friends, has been bought for eight hundred dollars by this lucky young lady," the auctioneer droned.

Because she and Tiffany had been talking, they had missed seeing who bid on the first man and won him.

"Hey, Number Two's about to make his way on stage." He did, and Tiffany groaned. "I'll have to pass."

Bridget rolled her eyes, only to feel shock at the number of women who bid on the second man, who was anything but handsome. He obviously came from the shallow end of the gene pool, but to her surprise he was sold for five hundred and fifty dollars.

The next dozen men passed in a whirl before Bridget's eyes. She was only called back to the moment by Tiffany's gasp.

"All right!" Tiffany cried. "Now *he's* more like it. Talk about stud material."

"God, Tiff, try to control yourself," Bridget muttered as her eyes migrated to the stage and settled on the man who was standing front and center. And looking at her.

Bridget gulped as their eyes met, feeling for the first time in her life as if she'd been hit with a stun gun. She wanted to move, to turn away, to *scream* if it would break the contact with this man.

It wasn't that he was all that good-looking. He wasn't. And while there was something about his tanned, uneven features and rock-hard body that *was* attractive, it was his green eyes and the way he looked at her that sent her senses into a tailspin.

No man, certainly not Hamilton, had ever appraised her in such a way, a way that was both exciting and frightening. Why on earth would this man be on an auction block? she asked herself, before giving in to the disgust that flooded through her.

What did she care? She had no intention of taking part in any of this crazy mess.

Then *his* eyes roamed over her.

"Do I hear a bid for Mr. Jeremiah Davis, ladies?"

As if her body had severed itself from her head, Bridget stood up and her mouth opened. "One thousand dollars!"

Three

—

"Going once, going twice," the auctioneer chanted, then pounded the gavel on the podium and shouted, "Sold! To the redheaded lady in the front row."

The crowd cheered and clapped at the same time Tiffany locked her fingers around Bridget's forearm and jerked her down to her seat.

"Have you lost your mind?"

At first Tiffany's screeching didn't penetrate the fog that surrounded Bridget's brain. In fact, she felt as if her entire body was encased in cement. Yet somehow she was able to pull her eyes off the man who was in the process of receiving a congratulatory slap on the back from the auctioneer.

"Do you know what you just did?" Tiffany screeched, though for Bridget's ears alone.

Bridget tried mentally to reach the heart that had dropped to somewhere around her toes, yank it in place and respond like the sane human being she knew herself to be. But she couldn't, even if everyone close by was giving them the once-over. Her tongue wouldn't move.

"I can't believe it!" Tiffany's eyes were wild as she stared at Bridget as though she was a stranger.

Still dazed, Bridget shook her head, then stared at her friend. "Did . . . did I just do what I think I just did?"

"Damn straight you did, you little idiot."

Bridget grabbed her stomach. "I think I'm going to be sick."

"It'd serve you right," Tiffany said, a twinkle settling into her eyes.

"You think this is funny?"

"Sure do, honey, especially after all that posturing in Houston. 'No way will I waste plane fare to this hick town, much less take part in any bidding.' Now what happens? You open your big mouth and insert your little foot!"

Bridget wailed, "What am I going to do?"

Tiffany grinned. "Well, friend, all I can say is that you've got your butt in a wringer. If it's any consolation, he's the best of the lot . . . by a *long* shot!"

"Don't torment me, please."

Tiffany erupted into laughter. "*Me* torment *you?* I think it's the other way around. You're the one who plopped down a cool thousand simoleons for the man."

Bridget had never felt so foolish in her entire life. She couldn't remember feeling like this even as a teenager, when she'd first discovered boys and giggled with her friends about them. Well, what was done, was done and while she couldn't undo it, she could fix it. Or at least, she hoped she could.

"What next?" Tiffany asked.

"Where is he?"

"By he do you mean your *hunk,* Mr. Jeremiah Davis?"

Bridget glared at Tiffany. "He's not *my* hunk. And yes, I mean him."

"Well, at the moment," Tiff drawled, "he's shooting the breeze with the other fellows offstage."

"Is he looking at me?"

"As a matter of fact, he is, and with quite a lot of curiosity, I might add."

"You're loving this, aren't you?"

"Yep. I want to see how the counselor at law handles this one."

Bridget considered strangling Tiffany on the spot, but the auctioneer chose that moment to rap his gavel. "That's it, ladies. You've made your choices, and in doing so, you've helped us collect thousands of dollars for the women's shelter. Now it's time for you winners to grab your men and join in the fun."

Everyone laughed and cheered—everyone except Bridget, who continued to sit in her chair, fearing if she moved, she would have a panic attack. She took several deep breaths and turned stricken eyes toward her friend, who also remained seated.

"So what are you going to do?" Tiffany asked in a bland tone.

Bridget wasn't fooled. Underneath that bland exterior, laughter ached to bubble through.

"I wish to God I knew."

Tiffany was loving every minute of her discomfort, but then well she should, Bridget thought. This served her right for acting holier than thou. Now she was having to choke on every word she'd said.

But more than that, what was she going to do about Jeremiah Davis, the man she had won? At any moment, she feared, he would walk up and say something to her. He *had* to think she was a sex-starved nympho. What if he made advances based on that assumption?

Tiffany voiced those exact thoughts. "I expect your man to appear on the scene at any second. And from the looks of him, he'll make you think of Hamilton as a fond memory. Jeepers, did you see the size of his hands? Not to mention several other parts?"

"I don't want to talk to him *or* his parts," Bridget responded in a strained voice, feeling the anxiety build inside her. Not a good sign. "I'll just pay my money, then we'll leave."

"Without saying anything to him?"

"Yes."

"Fat chance. That man, all these men, think they have the makings of a relationship with the women who won them. After all, that's what this was all about—someone to share their lives and their work." Tiffany chuckled.

"Well, you and he can *both* forget that. I don't know what happened to me, Tiff. I had no intention of saying a word."

"If I'd had any extra money, I would have snatched him up myself."

"You're welcome to him…and I didn't snatch him up!"

"Whatever you say, but a thousand dollars says you did. Argue with that! Look, I'm going to mingle, have something to drink and a bite to eat. You want to come?"

Bridget shook her head. "The thought of food makes me sick."

"Suit yourself, but I'm starving."

Bridget's panic flared anew. "You mean you're going to leave me? Alone?"

Tiffany's lips twitched. "Yeah, as a matter of fact, I am. The last time I checked, you were a big girl.

You've been dressing yourself for years now. Of course...you just bought yourself some help with the undressing.''

"I'll get you back, Tiffany Russell. Count on it."

Tiffany winked, then walked off.

Bridget was tempted to go with her friend, but she didn't think her legs would cooperate. They had as much consistency as water, which was what she needed to take a pill, her anxiety having reached a dangerous level. She dug in her purse, nabbed a tiny tablet and tossed it down cold turkey.

"Mind if I join you?"

She hadn't seen him coming, and though she'd known his appearance was inevitable, she wasn't prepared. Swallowing hard, she turned and looked into Jeremiah Davis's face.

Up close, he was even more intimidating and fascinating. He had to be well over six feet tall—she knew that because he was towering above her. Against that tanned skin, his sandy hair and mustache looked almost gold. But again, it was those piercing green eyes that were his best asset among uneven features.

"Why? Am I coming apart?" she asked, hoping the remark would make him keep his distance.

His lips twitched, as though he knew she was uncomfortable. Still, he lowered himself into the chair that Tiffany had vacated and plopped down the Stetson he'd had in his hand. That was when she smelled his cologne. Instead of being offensive, it evoked the same feeling inside her that she'd felt when he first swaggered onto that stage. Nor could she ignore the way his thighs filled out his jeans to perfection.

Something foreign had a stranglehold on her, and she jerked away from his gaze before she made a bigger fool of herself than she already had.

"So, want to tell me your name?" he asked, his voice sounding low and slightly rough around the edges. But then, *he* was rough around the edges in every respect. Still, she couldn't help but compare that voice to Hamilton's, whose precise vowels oftentimes sounded high and whiny. As for the men themselves, there was no comparison.

"Well?"

Realizing she hadn't answered his question, she cleared her throat and said, "It's Bridget Martin."

"You're not from around here, are you, Bridget Martin?"

"Actually, I'm from Texas."

He chuckled. "I sort of figured that. I love women with Southern drawls."

I bet you just love women, period, she thought, then wanted to kick herself for her cattiness. But more than that, for even caring if he'd slept with every woman he'd ever met.

"Did this sideshow bring you to these parts?"

Her eyes narrowed. "Do I hear contempt for what just went on?"

He eased back in the chair, then said, "Yep, you did."

"Then why did you participate?"

"I thought that was obvious. I need a woman."

Bridget sucked in her breath and without thinking looked at him. The way he was staring at her, she might have been the only woman in the world. Shaken, she jerked her eyes from his, but not before she saw his lips twitch again. He was toying with her, and loving every minute of it. But why? What had she ever done to him?

"Then I'm afraid there's been a mix-up. Just because I helped out a women's shelter doesn't mean I need a man," she managed to say, though the last part seemed to lodge in her throat.

"Of course not, ma'am. I'm sure you fly all over the United States, giving money away like this. It's probably a great tax deduction, not that I know personally. Still—"

If she could get her hands on Tiffany, she would strangle her for sure. But Tiffany wasn't around, and even if she was, Bridget couldn't depend on her to get her out of this mess. She alone was responsible for the quagmire she'd gotten herself into and would have to get herself out of.

"Look, would you excuse me for a moment?" Bridget didn't have to go to the ladies' room, but she wanted him to think she did. She had to have some space, some time to think. She feared where this conversation was leading, and she had to have ammunition to head it off. What she intended to do was find Tiffany and persuade her to leave. Of course, she would have to pay the money, but a check was quick and easy to write.

This cowboy would just have to buy an electric blanket if he wanted warm feet at night...provided his ranch had electricity.

Jeremiah stood at the same time she did. Tipping his Stetson, he said, "Sure thing."

Feeling her entire body turn red at the mocking note in his voice, she turned and somehow managed to take a few steady steps.

"I'll be waiting for you right here. We have a lot to talk about, you know. I'm glad you're from Texas. At least you'll know the difference between a Hereford and a Charolais."

Bridget stopped in her tracks, swallowed hard, but didn't dare turn around. Wrong. They didn't have *anything* to talk about! She had no intention of continuing this conversation. Still, she wouldn't give him the satisfaction of knowing that he'd struck a nerve. But he *did* know, and that galled her even more.

Damn him! What was a Charolais? She knew damned well Cadillac didn't make it.

Four

Jeremiah couldn't believe his good fortune. Hell, his mind was still reeling from the impact of what had happened. Having been down on his luck for so long with mounting bills, a dying cattle market and a decaying ranch, he wasn't about to look a gift horse in the mouth.

Yet a niggling thought in the back of his mind warned him that Bridget Martin didn't belong here, that something was not quite right. Her reaction when he'd mentioned Charolais cattle had set off an alarm.

She even looked out of place. She wasn't typical of the women who had shown up for the auction, an auction he still couldn't believe he'd taken part in. But that was another story altogether, one that was moot now that he had joined in this idiotic scheme.

It rankled, though, that he'd let his friends cajole him into taking part.

"Ah, come on, Davis, be a sport," one of the guys had said. "Hellfire, you're in the same shape as the rest of us, stuck here without womenfolk—and no hope of any ever being here unless we take matters into our own hands."

Drastic matters, Jeremiah had thought at the moment of that conversation, and his opinion hadn't changed. He still felt like the high school nerd who couldn't get a date.

But even as he ridiculed himself, he couldn't stop the unwanted and foreign sensations that invaded his insides as he watched Bridget Martin walk toward the ladies' room, her stride perfection in motion.

He knew he should turn away from the sight of her deliciously rounded buttocks and the way they filled out her jeans with no room to spare. He took a deep breath, endeavoring to calm his racing pulse.

What the hell was happening to him? He'd never reacted to a woman with such speed or sexual precision in his entire life, not even his wife, God rest her soul.

Jeremiah paused and wiped the sweat from his brow, even as Bridget disappeared behind the ladies' room door. Too bad his erotic thoughts didn't disappear, as well.

When he'd walked up to her and sat beside her, her perfume—delicate, like her—had slapped him in the face, though in retrospect it had actually been a caress.

At close range, she'd been breathtakingly lovely. She was fair-skinned, with short red hair that was kind of wild, but that, he assumed, was the latest style. It didn't matter, because it set off huge brown eyes, narrow cheekbones, a perfect nose and a slightly full lower lip that gave her mouth a sensual pout.

However, it was when she'd taken a shuddering breath, throwing her full breasts into prominence, that he'd felt that first sexual jolt, causing his head to spin. And not just his head, he'd been forced to admit. He'd felt the heat spin down into his lower body, and his jeans had tightened in certain areas. He'd wished then that he'd had *several* beers instead of just two.

He wished that same thing now as he watched her exit the rest room, looking miserable. But then, he was miserable, too, but for a different reason. Of that he was sure.

He cursed, then waited to see if she would walk toward him, expecting her to ignore him, then bolt. If she was smart, he told himself, she would do just that. This whole bizarre scene was out of touch with reality, yet for the moment, he didn't care. Bizarre or not, he didn't intend to let her disappear.

And it wasn't just because he was horny, either. Yeah, right, Davis, his conscience contradicted with intense scorn.

He paid it no attention as he strode toward her.

"How about something to drink?" he asked, struggling to come to grips with his out-of-control libido.

Her breath escaped in a rush even as she looked at him. "Look, Mr. Davis, I don't—"

"Why not be a sport? People drink things in Texas, don't they?"

"Of course, but I'm taking—"

"Hey, I know this is awkward as hell, but for the time being, let's pretend we're at a barbecue and that we just met under normal circumstances."

She didn't meet his eyes. "I don't think that's a good idea. We need to talk. You see, I have no—"

"If you're about to say what I think you are, then I need a beer. And you can have some punch. You owe me at least that much, since you outbid women who were *serious* about all this."

"Fair enough, Mr. Davis."

In spite of the fact that he knew in a short time he would never see her again, he chuckled. "Don't you think you'd best call me Jeremiah? After all, you paid a thousand dollars for the right."

Her face turned beet red, and when she spoke, her tone was curt. "For charity, not for you."

"Yeah, you keep reminding me of that. So how 'bout that drink?" he pressed, choosing to ignore her last statement, especially as it riled him a bit. Maybe he wouldn't let her off the hook so easily, after all. His gut told him that she had no intention of going through with this deal. Oh, he felt sure she would write the check to charity. If the truth be known, he would bet she could afford to write a check for a hell of a lot more. But that wasn't the point. Her holier-than-thou attitude rankled him big time.

Maybe he would make her squirm a little before she bolted, just as he was squirming now. The thought brought another smile to his lips.

"So, are you game? A cup of punch is mighty cheap payment for a thousand bucks."

"Oh, all right," she muttered, "but then we have to talk because . . . I have no intention—"

He wanted to grab her arm and tell her he got the message, but he restrained himself. Instead, he gestured that she should precede him, keeping his smile intact, though it was forced.

A few minutes later, he had a beer and she had a cup of punch. He had maneuvered them to a secluded place away from the band, the dancing and the food line. The atmosphere was far from quiet, but at least they didn't have to raise their voices to hear one another.

Jeremiah decided to make only small talk for now. "Your friend seems to be having a good time. She sure can dance."

Bridget turned and faced the crowded dance floor. "She'd rather dance than eat."

"What about you?"

"What about me?"

"Would you rather dance or eat?"

Her voice was husky, he noted, at the same moment she ran the tip of her tongue across that full lower lip.

She must have heard his sharp intake of breath, because for the second time that day, their eyes locked.

Against Jeremiah's will, his blood thickened. He fought to combat his growing passion, feeling out of control, something he despised and wouldn't tolerate. At the moment, however, he didn't know how to regain control.

"Neither one, but I'd like another glass of punch," she said.

He heard the desperate note in her voice and didn't argue. Hell, he needed another beer, too, but he wasn't going to have one. He needed to be in full control of his faculties, or he feared he might do something he would regret for the rest of his life—like kiss her until she begged him to stop.

Seconds later, when he returned with another full cup of punch, her eyes were again on her friend, who was teaching someone to dance Texas style, or at least something he'd never seen before and assumed came from Texas.

"What are they doing?" he asked, as she took the cup from him.

Their fingers touched, and he sucked in his breath, trying to haul his unruly senses back in line.

She seemed to read his thoughts. Her face flushed, and she took a quick gulp of her punch.

"Sure looks like they're having fun," he added.

"I...I should go. My head suddenly feels kind of—"

She broke off, then jerked her eyes away from his.

Even though the sun had dwindled, turning to twilight, he could still see the heat as it invaded her throat, which drew his attention to her V-necked shirt, then to her breasts, making him wonder if they were flushed, as well. He cursed silently.

"Come on, let's dance." He knew his tone was brusque, but he didn't give a damn. He was in bad shape.

"Why should we, Mr. Davis?"

Damned if he intended to beg! Still... "Because you flew all the way out here from Texas, you got caught up in the moment and now you're feeling like a fool. Because you *smell* good, you look good, and you're obviously not in any strut to find a man. But mainly because—"

"Oh, all *right!*"

He circled her arm with one hand, using his other to set the empty containers on the nearest picnic table, then guided her onto the cement floor beneath a metal roof.

At first she remained ramrod straight, looking beyond his shoulder. He wanted to shake her into compliance, but, of course, he didn't, as everyone around would then be witness to his frustrations, not that anyone was paying attention to them.

The music was slow, and most couples were locked in embraces that were worthy of the bedroom. He smirked. Apparently the other women who'd won their men were more than happy with their situation.

Not so Bridget Martin. She was still as stiff and un-cooperative as a board, even though they moved in perfect unison. Again, he couldn't imagine what had driven her to come here, to take part in something she obviously abhorred. But the question that nagged him even more was, what had attracted her to him enough to make her bid a grand?

"Bridget, relax a little, okay?" he asked.

"I . . . can't." Her voice cracked.

For a minute he cursed himself for making her take part in something she didn't want to. Then he thought better of it. Hell, she was a big girl. He wasn't forcing her to remain in his arms. If she chose to leave, he couldn't stop her.

Yet he didn't intend to make it easy. "Normally, I'd say let your hair down, but yours is too short for that," he muttered, noticing his voice had grown husky.

She lifted her head and gazed at him, her lips part-ing. It was then that he did something out of the blue. His hand touched an errant strand of hair and hooked it behind her ear.

"Don't," she whispered, flinching.

"Whoa, it's okay. You're as skittish as one of my cutting horses. You don't have to be. I won't hurt you."

To his utter amazement, her body slid against his, and he felt the jolt of that contact fire every nerve ending he possessed.

"I feel so funny," she whispered, looping her arm around his neck.

He chuckled close to her ear. "I always thought you Texans could hold your liquor. You just had a little too much of that spiked punch."

She smiled and sighed, then snuggled closer.

It had been a long time since he'd been aroused to such a fever pitch, and for an instant, he was at a loss as to what to do. Why tease himself? Her nipples had begun to poke into his chest, and while that drove him wild, he knew this was headed nowhere. He felt as though he'd just won the lottery, only he knew he hadn't even bought a ticket. This whole situation was too fantastic to believe; this *woman* was too fantastic to believe!

This was insane. No, that wasn't right. Dangerous. That was the word that came to mind. Hell, he was drunk himself, though not on booze.

He was drunk on this *woman,* a woman who didn't give a damn if he took another breath. She'd told him point-blank that she didn't need a man, that the thousand dollars was just for charity. He hadn't *seen* a thousand dollars in a long time, yet here he stood, dancing with someone to whom the money meant no more than a passing fancy.

Fool!

What was with this woman? She was dancing close now, like a second coat of paint, and he felt her hand leave his, then snake its way around his neck. Worse, her other hand began working its way down his back, ending up in the pocket of his jeans.

Double damned fool!

Five

She shifted, then moaned, yet couldn't seem to wake up. Something was on her lips, something hot and sweet, like heated honey. That same something turned insistent, nudging, teasing, until her mouth parted. Then it took its own slow time touring her lips before suddenly spearing inside, bringing that hot sweetness with it.

She moaned again, wanting the torture to end, only she didn't know how. She wanted to openly protest. She had to protest. That thought, though still fuzzy in her mind, was the catalyst she needed. Her eyes blinked open to find strong arms wrapped around her.

God, they felt good. How could she object when she was on fire and felt treasured at the same time, a feeling she had never experienced in her life? Was she dreaming? Of course she was. There were no arms around her. Even with her eyes open, *he* was a figment of her imagination.

But if that was so, why was she naked?
Naked!
How could that be? She had never slept naked in her life, so why should she start now? Then she felt some-one move next to her, and her eyes sprang open. Even in the moonlit darkness, she could see a man's face as it peered at her. *What was going on?*

She didn't think she'd spoken out loud, didn't think her tongue or her voice would work. Apparently there was no need for words. He seemed to know what she was thinking, because he whispered, "It's me, and everything's all right."

But it wasn't all right, not if she was naked in bed with a man—a man who was just as naked. Bridget moaned, shifting onto her back, but it took all her strength to do that much. What was wrong with her? Why couldn't she scream for him to move, for him to stop touching her? Or, better yet, why couldn't she bound out of bed and tell him to go to hell?

Because he was arousing her, that was why. What was going on? Was she drugged? Was she high on the feel of this man's body molded to hers? Or was it the touch of his hands as they traced over her body like he owned it, only stopping when he reached the damp-ness between her thighs?

She tried to swallow, but her mouth was too dry.

He moved. She knew then that what was happen-ing to her was no dream, but honest-to-God physical contact. But with whom? Had she lost her mind? No! Whoever was doing this to her, making her feel like this—mushy and aching inside—was the one who had lost his mind.

She wouldn't stand for this another minute. She was outraged! She had trusted him. But who *was* "him"? She couldn't think, not when a hard, callused hand was wandering over her. She squirmed, tried to object again, to cry out, to tell him to stop.

But he wouldn't let her go, wouldn't stop the brazen torture. "No...don't..." she cried, but it was a weak cry, without substance.

"Yes, I have to."

"What...are you doing?" But she knew, even as he cupped that aching spot between her legs. He was making her hotter and wetter.

"Exactly what you want me to do."

The voice sounded as thick and slurred as she knew hers to be. Although her eyes were open and she was awake, she couldn't focus, nor could she think.

"What...what are you doing?" she repeated, hearing the hysteria in her voice, but unable to do anything about it.

"Making love to you." The voice was soft, yet rough, and a trifle unfamiliar.

"But—"

"You want me to stop?"

Yes, her mind screamed, while her body screamed *no.* Her body won.

When she didn't speak, he whispered, "This is right. You want me, too—I know it." His voice was deep and insistent. "Stop thinking and just feel, feel how much *I* want *you.*"

That was when she felt him, full and turgid against her, forcing her to recognize that her body was pliable and not at all outraged.

His hands moved over her with an out-of-control urgency, beginning with her face, her neck, her shoulders, then down her arms to her waist and finally her thighs.

That was when he moved on top of her, his hunger evident in the burning brightness of his eyes and his harsh breathing. He rested his arms on either side of

her so as not to crush her with his weight while his lips
sank onto hers.

He raised his mouth at the same time that one hand
shifted between her thighs, where he fingered, touched
and pressed.

"Oh, please!" she cried out, writhing.

"Oh, baby, baby," he countered, driving inside her.

She gasped, even as she welcomed his length, his
hardness, her insides rocking with sweetly savage intensity. Her fingernails dug into his back, and this time
he groaned, which both flamed their muted desire and
fueled their impatience.

He thrust deeper and harder. She held him as he
trembled above her, felt his every tremor as he thrust
again and again. Her body arched under his, so as not
to miss any contact with the hard, rough body ad-
hered to hers.

Then he slowed the pace, shifting to look at her, his
eyes glazed, using one hand to caress her, finding her
ripe, swollen breasts. She knew he was trying to make
it last, grasping a nipple between two fingers and tug-
ging on it.

Her stomach muscles contracted, binding him
tighter inside her while she pressed toward him again.
Still he prolonged the ecstasy, prolonging it until it
became agony.

"It's okay, honey," he ground out. "Don't fight it."

"Ohhhhh!" She erupted then, in a frenzy, locking
her legs around him in a scissorlike grip.

"Yes, oh, yes, that's it. Slow and easy."

She cried from deep within, even as another ripple
of pleasure rocked her. But when it was over, she realized in her fog-filled mind that he was still hard, that
he hadn't climaxed. With that thought in mind, she
blew on his ear, then probed the delicate inside with
her tongue.

"Oh, baby," he whispered, even as she felt his heart begin to pound.

But it was when she moved her hand to his buttocks and dug her fingers into the tense muscles that he went wild. He thrust faster and faster. His actions, combined with the continued throbbing inside her, gave her the strength to meet his demands. And when he climaxed, so did she, their bodies shuddering and clinging together.

Still, she didn't let go, nor did he, each savoring the feel of the other. Then the heat started over again. And the craving. His hands, his lips, his body made it happen all over again, and they trembled as one as the aftershocks rippled through.

An aching feeling had invaded her lower limbs, a strange weakness. Bridget tried to open her eyes, but failed. They wouldn't cooperate; they felt as if they had been glued together. Then she moved. Her eyes opened at the same time that her body winced.

She tried to bring some moisture to her dry, tender mouth. When her tongue touched it, she winced again, aware at the same time that her body felt the same way—tender and aching.

Had something happened that she didn't know about? Had she had a good time and missed out on it? Her lips and her body told her that she had.

She stared at the ceiling, trying to get her bearings. Nothing was familiar. She didn't know what made her turn. Maybe it was just the logical thing to do, finding herself in strange surroundings.

A man lay beside her—uncovered and naked as the day he'd come into the world—the man she had bid on and won. Jeremiah Davis. No! Her mind rebelled when the events of the day and night before came crashing down on her. She wanted to cry out. She

wanted to lunge out of the bed and run. She did neither, for fear of waking the stranger beside her.

Stranger!

Had she actually thought that word? Well, he might
be a stranger in every other way, but not where her
body was concerned. In that moment every detail of
what happened between them flashed to the forefront
of her mind—memories of heat, warmth and passion; of shadowy bodies locked and merging; of feverish words and slick skin, and the moist, pulsing
power of possession . . .

She stifled a cry. No! She wouldn't think about it.
Only she couldn't stop herself. The memories were like
a disease that had attached itself to her and was eating away at her insides.

It had all started on that damned dance floor. Actually it had started when she drank that punch, not
knowing until it was too late that it was spiked. Mix-
ing alcohol with her medication for her panic attacks
was a no-no. But in her own defense, she hadn't
known the punch had been doctored until she'd
slumped against Jeremiah and clung to him like a love-
starved teenager.

Yet there had been moments of rationality during
those many slow dances, moments when she'd tried to
keep him at bay, only it hadn't worked.

"I should go," she had whispered, hiccupping, then
giggling.

"Oh, I don't know about that," he'd responded, his
tone husky as he leaned over, brushing her neck with
his tongue.

"Stop that!" she'd gasped, another kind of panic
flaring through her. "You have no right!"

He'd regarded her with narrowed eyes, then chuckled. "Oh, I think I do, especially when every inch of

your body is propped against me. Your hand's been on
my butt for an hour now.''

"Er... I didn't mean—'' Bridget's tongue stumbled over the words.

"Shh, stop talking,'' he said, his warm breath fan-
ning her face, while a hand eased down and cupped
the cheeks of *her* buttocks, drawing her even closer to
him.

"Oh, please,'' she pleaded, aware that she had
completely lost control of herself and her emotions.

He kissed her then, the first of many hot, moist,
deep kisses that had sent her senses whirling even
more. Then there had been that confrontation with
Tiffany, a confrontation that was still fuzzy in her
mind, though she tried her best to remember.

She blocked another cry, knowing that her friend
was probably worried out of her mind about her; it
was daylight, and she wasn't in the motel where she
should have been.

Tiffany was going to kill her, because she'd warned
her. That much Bridget did remember.

"Have you lost your mind or what?'' Tiffany had
all but shouted at her after Bridget had left Jeremiah
and stumbled into the rest room.

"I don't know what you're talking about,'' she'd
replied, thick-tongued.

"The hell you don't. Not only is *he* mauling you—
you're mauling him in return. Do you know where
your *hands* have been?''

"I haven't... they haven't...''

"How would you know? You're tipsy.''

Bridget giggled. "So why don't *you* get tipsy and
have a good time?''

Tiffany snorted. "I'm going to the motel. Are you
coming with me or not?''

"No, she's coming with me.''

Both women turned and saw Jeremiah standing in the doorway of the women's room. Bridget giggled, then said, "Oops!"

Tiffany looked at Jeremiah and asked, "Can I depend on you to take care of her?"

"You bet," he responded without hesitation.

She turned to Bridget. "I'll see you at the motel. Later."

Well, later had never come. And yes, Tiffany would kill her, or at least make her wish she was dead. But then, she already wished that herself.

Bridget licked her dry lips and sneaked another look at Jeremiah. Thank God, he was still asleep. Should she try to creep out? Fear held her captive, but fear of what she didn't know.

She lay unmoving, with only her torrid thoughts for company as she remembered another fragmentary moment from last evening. Someone had shouted to them on the dance floor as the party neared an end. "Hey, let's go across the line and see what kind of trouble we can stir up."

Someone else shouted, "Yeah, let's take our new lady friends and show 'em how to gamble."

Somehow she and Jeremiah had ended up in the back of a van, where they'd huddled under a blanket and he'd held her tightly in the darkness, then kissed and fondled her until she ached all over. Her shirt had unbuttoned itself somehow, and her bra had seemed all out of place. His hands had kept busy, taking her breath away.

"Hey, you two lovebirds," a man cried out with laughter, "there's old Reagan Brewer's marriage chapel."

Another voice chimed in, "Want us to stop and let you two get hitched?"

Laughter rocked the van.

Bridget stared wild-eyed at Jeremiah.

"Want to?" Jeremiah whispered for her ears alone.

"Are you crazy?" she asked, her voice slurred even as she pushed her nipples harder against his hand.

He looked at her for a long moment, then said, "Yeah, probably. But then I think that goes for both of us."

Before she could reply, he sank his lips onto hers. From then on, until they reached this room, the evening was a complete blur.

Now, as she corralled her thoughts once again, Bridget went rigid. She couldn't think about last night anymore or she would go stark raving mad.

Suddenly she felt movement beside her. Even though her panic increased, she couldn't stop her eyes from seeking his.

He sat up, gazed at her, then grinned a lazy grin. "Good morning, *Mrs. Davis.*"

Bolting upright, Bridget stared at him in wild-eyed horror.

Six

Mrs. Davis!

What was he talking about? Bridget's head tilted, then reeled, and for a moment she thought she might lean over and empty the contents of her stomach. She'd heard him wrong, or else she was going insane.

Several deep, gulping breaths helped the oncoming nausea, but they did nothing to alleviate her chaotic mind.

"Well, aren't you going to say anything?" he asked, one eyebrow quirked.

She tried to swallow, but there wasn't enough saliva for even that reflex action.

As if sensing her difficulty and her shock, his features turned serious. "You don't remember, do you?"

"I remember enough," she lied, "to know that *you're* lying." Bridget clutched the sheet to her breasts as if it was her protection and lifeline.

Jeremiah's face turned a shade darker, and his tone was rough. "Just so you'll know for future reference, I don't lie."

"Why did you call me Mrs. Davis, then? Were you trying to be funny?"

He cursed, then gave her a sarcastic smile. "Sure thing, Bridget. Marriage is something I always kid around about."

"Only we're not married," she responded in a flat and unemotional tone, though her heart was pounding so hard in her chest that he was bound to hear it. He was still too damn close to her. Why didn't he get out of the bed? Why didn't she? Sudden tears pricked her eyes; she bit down on her lip and shifted her gaze.

"Wrong again, Mrs. Davis."

Another surge of nausea hit her, and this time she wasn't sure she could ward it off. She must have looked green, because concern replaced his hard expression.

"You all right?"

She took another deep breath and then, ignoring that concern, glared at him. "I don't believe we're married." She knew the desperate note in her voice was evident, but she didn't care. She had never felt more desperate in her life, and if she didn't take her medicine soon, she would have a full-blown panic attack. "I would remember if I'd done such a stupid thing."

Jeremiah's eyes took on a hostile glitter. "You don't believe me? Fine. But you can't argue with this!"

He reached over and grabbed a piece of paper off the table beside the bed. Before she could react, he stuck it in her face. "Have a long look. This is a marriage license, and guess whose names are on it?"

Bridget's initial reaction was to slap his gloating face, but something stopped her. Common sense, she suspected later, though at the time she'd had little of that or any other rational impulse. Maybe it was the warning that jumped into those already hostile eyes that made her realize this was no figment of her imagination, nor was it a game.

Her heart hammered, and the clenching in her stomach got worse. Turning, she saw her purse on the floor beside her. Without so much as looking at the paper, she reached inside her purse, retrieved a tiny pill, then swallowed it.

"What is that for?"

"I don't have to explain anything to you."

He gave her another mocking smile. "Where I come from, wives usually let their husbands in on their secrets."

"Stop saying that! I'm not your *wife!*" The words came out twenty decibels louder than her normal voice.

"Read the paper, dammit!"

Without looking at him, she did just that. Seconds later, she gazed at him, feeling as though someone had hit her with a baseball bat.

"Well, now are you convinced that I'm telling the truth? It's there in black and white."

"You took advantage of me, damn you! You knew I was drinking and didn't know what I was doing."

"The hell you didn't!" Jeremiah shot back. "No way you'll ever convince me you didn't know what you were doing when you climbed on top of me last night!"

Aghast, Bridget felt the color drain from her face, leaving her pale and shaking. "Why... you bastard!"

He laughed. "Believe me, honey, I've been called worse and survived."

Ignoring that, Bridget cried, "This is all a terrible mistake, and I want out, you hear? I want *out!*"

"No way, baby." His mouth was a grim line. "When you signed that piece of paper, you made a bargain—for better or worse. And I'll do whatever it takes to see that you honor it. You hear that?"

"Go to hell!"

He didn't say anything, and for a moment she thought she had gone too far. It took all her will-power not to draw away. But his only reaction was to throw back his head and laugh again, another rough, bitter laugh. Finally he climbed out of the bed.

She gasped when she realized again that he was na-ked. Only now, all that was visible was his muscled backside. She wanted to avert her gaze. She didn't want to watch the swagger of those hips and but-tocks. But more than that, she didn't want to remem-ber how she had dug her fingers into him as he'd thrust....

Only the slamming of the bathroom door in the hall aborted that train of thought. Groaning, Bridget wilted against the sheets, then yanked the cover over her head. But nothing could stop her mind from working. She no longer had the luxury of letting her emotions dominate. She had to achieve a rational mind-set. While this man might be a country bump-kin, he was no fool. He had that piece of paper to prove it.

She began shaking all over, then took several deep breaths. No longer did she fear having a panic attack; the medication would keep that at bay. What she did fear, however, was the inability to take control of her emotions and get back her life as she'd known it be-fore she came to this hole-in-the-wall part of the country.

When she saw Tiffany, there would be hell to pay. *Tiffany!* Oh, God, she must be out of her mind wondering what had happened to her.

Bridget groaned again, knowing that she would have to make that dreaded phone call to her friend, but what she would say didn't bear thinking about. But then, if Tiffany was worried, it served her right.

"It's your fault I'm here in the first place," Bridget muttered.

She couldn't think about Tiffany, not now, anyway. What she did have to think about was how she was going to get herself out of this mess. No matter what Jeremiah said, he couldn't force her to stay with him, married or not, she reasoned. Or could he? At the moment, she was at his mercy.

Forget that.

She was overreacting. She wasn't at his mercy. She wasn't at any man's mercy—not her daddy's; not Hamilton's and not any of the men at her office. Hadn't she proved that?

In fact, she had worked hard to maintain her independence, and she wasn't about to forfeit it now. She'd vowed long ago not to be like her mother, who'd let her husband dominate her life. That was one of the reasons Bridget had filed the sexual harassment suit.

No, she had to be as strong now as she'd been then. Granted, she had made a mistake, the first of which was drinking any of that punch. She hadn't known it was spiked, but she should have assumed it was. Maybe she hadn't cared. Maybe she'd already been drunk on that cowboy who only had to look in her direction to make her insides melt.

Well, that was yesterday, and this was today. Harsh reality had certainly jerked a knot in her sexual fantasies. Now all she wanted was to leave with as much of her dignity intact as she could muster.

She reminded herself of another mistake, though nothing that a court of law couldn't correct—even a Utah court. Or had they been married in Nevada? And she wasn't licensed in either state! What a mess, but all wasn't lost. She could get permission to handle it *pro hac vice,* without taking a bar exam.

No. The best move was to just get up, get dressed and get back to Houston.

To what?

Bridget's heart sank. She had left behind as many or more problems than she had facing her now. Her parents weren't speaking to her; she had no job; Hamilton was being his usual pain-in-the-backside self.

So what was she saying to herself? That she should stay here? She sucked in her breath and held it. Maybe that was the answer. Why *not* stay, at least for a while? She needed a place to nurse her wounds, to heal her body and mind and to regain her self-confidence, which was sagging in spite of her rallying thoughts of a moment ago.

Had she gone completely off the deep end?

No, but what she had done was lose her ability to function as she should in the courtroom, and that scared the hell out of her. Since she had been diagnosed with the acute anxiety that caused her panic attacks, the thought of facing a courtroom atmosphere was intolerable. Until she overcame that fear, she wouldn't be worth anything to herself or to her profession.

And there was a charm about this godforsaken place that fascinated her. Still, her volatile relationship with this stranger couldn't possibly work, no matter how much she needed a place to hide.

So the marriage and the hunk would have to go. That thought brought peace to her heart and a smile to her lips.

With that thought in mind, Bridget tossed back the covers, sat up, then reminded herself through clenched teeth, "Now, all you have to do is tell him."

Jeremiah watched as the yellow center of the egg broke in the pan and ran. "Dammit," he muttered, thinking this was the first time in eons he'd broken an egg yolk.

But then, that wasn't the only thing he'd broken. He'd lost his mind by pulling the craziest stunt of his entire life—marrying that dizzy broad in the next room.

Damn!

The worst part about the whole charade was that he hadn't been drinking, or at least not enough that he hadn't known what he was doing.

When one of the guys in the van had hollered out about pulling into the wedding chapel, especially as they all knew the justice of the peace who owned and operated it, he'd said okay. But he hadn't been responsible for his actions, not with the taste of Bridget's sweet kisses on his lips and the burgeoning fullness of her breasts in his hands.

After that, one thing had led to another, and he was a married man. God! His hands shook so for a moment that he had to set the spatula down. Unable to look at that egg another second, he took the pan from the burner and set it in the sink, then walked to the window and stared out at the mountains beyond, begging for the peace of mind they always brought.

No such luck today.

Hell, he couldn't even see the mountains; he could only see Bridget's face as it had looked last night in the moonlight, bathed in sweat as she sat atop him and rode him like a wild filly until their frenzy wilted into utter exhaustion.

Lowering his head, he gripped the cabinet so hard he felt his knuckles pop. But the only pain he felt was in his gut. He'd sworn when Margaret died that he would never remarry. Heaven help him, he'd intended to stick to that vow.

But when he'd seen Bridget yesterday, then felt her body against his on the dance floor and later in the van, something had snapped inside him, something foreign and animalistic.

"Hell, you could have just taken her to bed," he muttered. "You didn't have to marry her, for Pete's sake!"

He *had* married her, though, and for reasons other than wanting to sleep with her. He just wasn't prepared to face or deal with those reasons at the moment. There would be time enough for that later.

Right now, he had to figure out how he was going to get through the next confrontation with her. What he ought to do was let her go. That would be the smartest and most logical thing. Even if she wanted to stay under his roof, it wouldn't work out.

She was from a different world. Even though he didn't know a damn thing about her, he wasn't blind. She was rich; he would bet his last breath on that. She was also self-assured and could hold her own against any man.

Yet everything inside him rebelled at letting her walk out of this house. He didn't understand why, either, unless it really was sheer physical desire that made him want to hold on to her. He'd heard about that kind of burning obsession, about what it could do to a man's nerves and how it could distort his judgment. He'd never experienced it, though, until last night—until Bridget Martin.

Jeremiah had *never* responded so strongly to anyone in his life, nor had anyone ever responded that way toward him. He could see Bridget, could feel her nails digging into his buttocks. She'd given her all, held nothing back, which had made him do the same.

He cursed, feeling a betrayal to his dead wife so acute that he wanted to beat the hell out of the cabinet with his bare fist. But he knew that wasn't the answer. The answer was to let Bridget have her freedom, chalk last night up to a fantasy and get the hell on with his life.

Yeah, he'd do that. He'd tell her that she was right, that what happened was not only insane, but a farce. Maybe he could call up old Reagan, get him to tear up the license, maybe just void it before things went any further. Besides, *his* feelings weren't the only ones he had to consider. He had—

"Jeremiah?"

So deep in thought was he that he had no idea his privacy had been invaded until he heard the husky voice.

He swung around and stared at the woman who was now his wife and knew with a certainty born of old that he could never willingly let her go.

Seven

She wanted to say something, but when she opened her mouth, nothing came out. Her senses were swamped once again by the animal attraction this man held for her. She'd never reacted to anyone this way.

Not only did that fact amaze her, it mortified her, as well. Yet she couldn't seem to pull her eyes off him.

He had showered, and his longish hair was still wet. Droplets of water were trapped in its sandy thickness, making it appear darker than it was. He was dressed as he'd been last evening, except he wore a different shirt—a dark green one. His close-fitting jeans, though, were the same ones.

Suddenly murky memories of him ripping off his clothes and baring his chiseled but well-developed body, then thrusting his hot hardness inside her, blindsided her.

Lowering her head, Bridget strove to control her perverse thoughts.

"Mornin'."

The raspy tone of his voice brought her head up. His eyes were intent and disturbing as they roamed over her.

Against her will, Bridget's nerves tightened even more. But she had to be strong. She couldn't let the tension between them make her more foolhardy than she'd already been. "No matter what you say, you can't hold me here against my will."

Even though she'd made up her mind to hang around the village, so to speak, she had to get out of this house and away from him ASAP.

"You're right, I can't."

She was taken aback, not expecting him to acquiesce so quickly. But then, what *had* she expected? She almost smiled at the answer that jumped to the forefront of her mind. For a second there she'd envisioned him using some kind of caveman tactic, forcing her to stay, which was ludicrous. He might be rough around the edges, but instinct told her that he would never hurt her.

After the first frenzy of their desperate coupling had come to an end last night, she couldn't have asked for anyone to be more tender and conscious of her needs. She felt a blush flood her face and turned away.

"You want some coffee?"

She jerked her head around, then swallowed hard. He was leaning against the cabinet, arms folded over his chest, staring at her. She saw the light in his eyes and was aware that he knew what she'd been thinking. She fought the urge to slap his smug face.

"No, thank you." Her reply came out stiff and rather squeaky.

He shrugged. "Suit yourself. But I'm going to finish mine. Can't get going in the mornings without my pusholine."

He lifted the mug to his lips, and when he did, he tipped his head back. Her eyes targeted his throat and the movement of his Adam's apple. For a moment it appeared as if he was having difficulty in swallowing. Or was she just mesmerized by his throat? By *him?*

Dampness flooded the juncture of her thighs. Had she really run her tongue over that same throat last night? Had she clung to him, touched him, then let his mouth probe every intimate inch of her body?

"It won't work, you know." She heard the desperation in that statement. Who was she trying to convince, anyway, him—or herself? To make matters worse, he hadn't even mentioned it working. He'd admitted he couldn't or wouldn't hold her to this farce of a marriage. Hadn't he?

"Oh, I don't know so much about that." His eyes, which probed hers, were deep set and sensual. "Seems to me we have a lot in common."

Her heart pounded.

"And you know it." His voice had dropped another octave, and she ached to counterattack with words, but she couldn't, because what he said was true. Still, she wasn't about to let him have the last word.

She lifted her head. "It was just sex. Nothing more, nothing less."

"And you don't think that's important?" he asked with raised eyebrows.

"Maybe, but sex without anything else has no staying power."

"Well, who's to say we can't work on the anything else and get that staying power?"

Oh, Lord, instead of bringing this foolishness to a close with as much dignity as the situation would allow, then making her escape, she was just digging the hole deeper.

"It won't work," she stressed, hearing the weakness in her voice, then flinching inwardly.

He grinned. "How do you know till you've tried? It worked pretty well last night...better than just pretty well, in fact."

"Look—"

"Besides," he continued as if she hadn't spoken, "I need a woman around the place, and you're that woman."

Her jaw sagged. Now the caveman tactic she'd feared a while ago was rearing its ugly head. "I don't get it. Why did you have to resort to this crazy junction to get a woman? I mean you're..." Her voice trailed off.

She couldn't believe she was asking him such a question. She was paying him a compliment. She didn't care why he'd participated. It was none of her business. Just turn around and leave, she told herself. That was the business she ought to be about, and nothing else.

Yet she didn't move.

"I'm what? Good in bed?"

She sucked in her breath, then stretched her lips into an angry line. "That wasn't what I was going to say, damn you! Just forget last night, okay? It was a mistake."

"Are you sure about that?" he taunted with a smile that was nothing short of a smirk.

She bypassed both the taunt and the smile and said with forced bluntness, "Surely, there's someone in a neighboring town who you could've met and developed a relationship with."

"It's not that easy. It's remote here, and not many women want to leave civilization to come here."

"So are you saying that you've never had—" She broke off; she'd been about to veer onto another dangerous track.

"A relationship?" he finished for her, then paused and gulped down the last of his coffee. He slammed the cup onto the cabinet, then added flatly, "No, I'm not saying that at all. Actually, I'm a widower."

"A widower," she mimicked, feeling shocked when she shouldn't have.

His features turned dark, as did his eyes. "My wife died three years ago."

"How...I mean she must've been young."

"She had a heart attack. Heart trouble ran in her family."

"I'm sorry."

"So am I." His tone was brooding.

Tension and unsaid words quivered in the air between them as their eyes met and held. Things were going from bad to worse, and still she didn't move. Instead, she licked her lips, then asked, "Did you—"

"Enough about me," he cut in, his eyes focused on her lips.

Her breath escaped in a rush as she picked up on that look. But before she could say or do anything, he continued, "What about you? You ever been married?" He paused, and his features darkened. "Or perhaps you're already married."

"Of course, I'm not married," she snapped.

"Oh, yes, you are," he countered, his tone soft. "You just don't wanna be." Following a short, loaded silence, he added, "So what do you do back in..." He waited for her to fill in the blank.

"Houston. That's my home." This conversation was giving new meaning to the word "insanity." She had spent the night in this man's arms, with him buried inside her for the majority of that night. Yet neither of them knew one damn thing about each other except for... Not only was that demented, but dangerous, as well, especially since she was fairly sure he hadn't used any protection.

At that thought, Bridget's heart faltered. She should ask, but she would rather cut her tongue out. Later. She would ask that question at another time.

"Is there someone back home, someone special?"

She shook her head to clear it. "Yes and no."

He reached over, lifted the pot and poured himself another cup of coffee. "That's rich. Just how the hell am I supposed to interpret that?"

"You aren't. It's none of your concern."

Jeremiah's jaw tightened, but he didn't say anything else, for which she was thankful. Feeling her legs shake, she eased into the nearest dining room chair and, taking advantage of the lull in the conversation, gazed about her. The kitchen was bright; the walls were painted yellow and the cabinets white. Her eyes settled on a basket of fake flowers for a second before moving to the buffet strewn with papers and knick-knacks.

While the room had obviously known a woman's touch, something, nevertheless, was lacking, Bridget thought. It had an air of neglect, of sadness, which brought a twinge to her heart.

"So what do you do back in big old Houston, Texas?"

He'd caught her off guard once more, which seemed to be his forte. His voice sounded almost pleasant, and the tension eased somewhat.

"I'm a practicing attorney."

He whistled, then took another swig of his coffee.

"You're shocked," she said.

His eyes mocked her once again as he looked her up and down, his gaze resting longer on her breasts.

In spite of herself, Bridget's stomach clenched.

"Yeah, you could say that. I've never known any big-city attorney who dressed in jeans and boots."

She forced herself to relax, though she dared not look at him. First, she wanted to ask just how many attorneys he'd known, then decided against it. While he might live in an unpopulated area, he wasn't dumb, nor was he uneducated. Instinct told her that. Second, she wanted to admit that she was as uncomfortable in this getup as she looked, but she held her tongue on that account, as well. She had no intention of telling him anything about her personal life. She suspected he wasn't about to confide in her, either.

Still, she had to ask the question that had been gnawing at her and continued to do so. "Why did you do it—marry me, I mean?" Her voice quivered. "You knew I'd had too much to drink, that I wasn't in my right mind."

"You really don't remember any of it?"

"Only someone hollering out and asking if he should stop at some chapel."

"That's about the size of it. Then one thing led to another."

"Only you weren't drunk, were you?"

"No."

"Damn you!" she cried.

"Don't yell at me. Why the hell did you come here, anyway?"

"On a lark...a dare, actually."

He spat out an explctive. "So you had no intention of taking part in the auction?"

Her face turned red. "Of course not."

"Then why did you?"

"I haven't the foggiest idea. I can only attribute it to a momentary loss of sanity."

This time *his* face turned red. "Then we've got a real problem here, 'cause as you well know, getting a woman was my sole purpose for letting my friends talk me into participating in that auction."

"Which is the craziest and most medieval thing I've ever heard. Surely none of you thought these women might be serious?"

"Of course they were serious. They're apparently needy, too, in their own way. You seem to be the exception." He paused, appraising her once again. "Not everyone in the world is a spoiled socialite who has everything she wants handed to her on a silver platter."

"How dare you say that?" Bridget asked. "You don't know anything about me!"

"I know enough from what you just said that you don't give a damn or know a thing about how the other half lives. You might have thought this was a lark, but the men in this community were sincere."

"What about you? I don't believe for a minute that you wanted to take part in that auction until your friends talked you into it."

He paled, and she knew she had struck a nerve. Good. He hadn't expected anything to come of this, only he was too chicken to admit it.

He walked closer and stood over her, his mouth stretched in a tight line. "It looks like we've both stepped in manure over our heads, but that doesn't change things. In the eyes of God and the laws of the State of Nevada, we're married." He paused again, while his thumb traced a sensuous path down her shoulder.

She ignored the ache his touch created within her as he went on, "So, until we figure out what we're going to do about that, I suggest you make yourself at home. I have a herd I need to tend to."

With that, he turned and stomped toward the door.
A herd! He had to see about the herd. Hysteria
bubbled through her, followed by tears. What had she
gotten herself into? What had she done?

"Jeremiah!"

He swung around, his face hard. "What?"

"I . . . I have to know. Did . . . did you use any—"

He seemed to read her thoughts. Again. His face
softened for a moment. "No, but you don't have to
worry. I haven't been with a woman since my wife
died."

He walked out, slamming the door behind him. A
sob caught in Bridget's throat just as the phone rang.
She reached for a tissue in her pocket and placed it
against her eyes. Should she answer it? she asked herself, fighting for control.

Tiffany! It could be her friend chasing her down.
Without thinking any further, she jumped up and
reached for the phone.

"Davis residence," she whispered.

"Thank God!"

Bridget breathed an audible sigh of relief. "Tiff, I
knew it would be you."

"I'm sure you have something to tell me, right?"

"You don't want to know."

"The hell I don't! Tell me what's going on."

Bridget sat down before she fell down. "I'm on
Jeremiah Davis's ranch. But you already knew that."

"How long have you been there?"

Silence.

"Bridget!"

"All night," she responded in a small voice.

"And you slept on the couch, of course?"

Bridget's stomach hollowed, but she didn't let her
friend's condemnation get to her. Besides, Tiffany was
right. "You don't want to know that, either."

"No, you're right, I don't. Have you lost your ever-lovin' mind?"

"I had too much to drink."

"Don't I know it! And the worst part is, I haven't seen you take a drink in a long time. What demon possessed you last night?"

Jeremiah Davis had possessed her.

"Come on Bridget, 'fess up. What really happened?"

Bridget hadn't told Tiffany about her panic attacks or the medication she was taking. That was something too personal and too embarrassing to share, even with her best friend.

"The punch was spiked, and I didn't know it," Bridget said, her tone lame, at best. "You know I can't hold liquor."

"Hell, I should've jerked you by the hair of your head out to the car when I had the chance." Tiffany was quiet for a minute. "Don't you know you're playing with fire, that—"

Bridget stopped her. "It's okay. *He's* okay."

"Is that what he said?"

"Yes."

"And you believe him?"

Bridget didn't hesitate. "Yes, I do."

"You're hopeless, and I'm wasting my time trying to talk to you."

"Look, Tiff, there's something else I have to tell you, but you have to promise not to say a word to anyone, least of all my parents."

"I'm listening." Tiffany's voice was without emotion as if she'd reached her limit.

"I'm . . . we got married last night."

"Oh, my God! Are you nuts?"

"Shh, don't holler," Bridget pleaded. "Someone might hear you."

"Who would that be? There's no one anywhere near me in this fleabag motel."

"Tiff, please, just go back home."

"Without you?" Tiffany's tone was incredulous.

"Yes, for the time being."

"What are you going to do?" Tiffany sounded dazed.

Bridget's hand clenched the receiver. "Figure out a way to undo this mess, I suppose. I can't just walk off with a legal husband in the State of Utah!"

"Well, God help you is all I can say," Tiffany responded in a deflated voice.

"I'll be in touch, okay?"

"You sure you won't reconsider and go back with me? *Now?*"

Bridget took a steadying breath. "Wish me luck, okay?"

"Honey, you're going to need more than luck."

"Don't, please. It's bad enough."

"Then do something about it! Hellfire, you're an attorney. He can't hold you to that farce of a marriage—not if you don't want him to, that is."

Bridget didn't say anything.

Tiffany sighed. "All I can say is, he must have something fantastic behind that zipper!"

With that, Tiffany hung up, leaving Bridget staring at the receiver, her face red and her heart pumping overtime.

Eight

"Every tongue in this entire county is flapping."

Jeremiah's brows pinched together in a dark frown as he stared at his old friend Irma Quill, who ran the local grocery store, café, library and sundry other businesses.

"About *me?* Is that what you're saying?"

"Don't sound so shocked and innocent. You know very well it's about you."

Irma was a tiny, birdlike woman with a mind as sharp as her wit. One could forgive her that sharpness, or anything else, for that matter, especially when she smiled. That smile, along with twinkling deep blue eyes whose color hadn't begun to fade despite her being in her late sixties, made everyone feel special.

And Jeremiah felt luckier than most. He was her pet, more so after his wife had died.

"Got any fresh veggies you don't need?"

Irma made a face, then got up and with her usual jerky movements crossed to the cabinet and poured two cups full of coffee. Once she sat down at the kitchen table in the apartment in back of the shop where she'd long resided alone as a widow, she glared at her visitor.

"You know I have all the veggies *you* could eat," she snapped.

Jeremiah didn't take offense at her sharp tone. He smiled, though his smile didn't last long. "Okay, Irm, what's on your mind?"

She made another face. "It's not what's on my mind that counts. It's what's on yours. You didn't come into town at dawn to talk about the veggies in my freezer or the ones growing in the garden."

"You're right, I didn't," Jeremiah said, taking off his Stetson and tossing it onto the nearest chair. "Since you just told me that tongues are wagging, I guess you know why I'm here."

Irma took a sip of her coffee. When she did, Jeremiah couldn't help but notice that the liquid wasn't much darker than Irma's tanned skin, which showed how many hours she spent in her garden.

"I'd rather hear it from you, son, than old lady Swanson, who thrives on keeping her nose up someone else's you-know-what."

Jeremiah chuckled. "Lordy, you mean even *she's* heard about it?"

"Huh, she may claim she's deafer than a post, but don't believe a word of it. She hears anything she wants to." Irma gestured impatiently. "Enough about that old bag. I want to know if the wagging tongues are right."

For a second Jeremiah didn't respond. He took several swigs of his coffee and wished it was laced with something strong, something that would help get the kink out of his gut. But drinking wasn't the answer to his unsolved problems. He'd found that out when Margaret died. That was one of the reasons his aunt had...

"Jeremiah, stop stalling. Come clean. It's good for the soul."

He shook his head, relieved that Irma had cut into his thoughts, though he didn't think the past was any less painful than the present. His lips thinned, and his tone was belligerent when he said, "Okay, I got married last night."

Irma moaned, then her eyes sparked. "Too bad you're too old and too big for me to yank you across my knee and beat the living daylights out of you."

"I'm afraid it's too late for that."

"So were you drinking?"

"I'd only had a few beers."

"You mean you had all your wits about you when you did it?"

Jeremiah looked his friend straight in the eye. "I knew exactly what I was doing."

"You can't be serious!"

"The minute I saw her, I knew I had to have her."

Irma's chapped lips fell open. "But marriage? Nowadays, I thought you could pretty much get the milk without buying the cow."

Jeremiah lunged to his feet and glared at Irma. "Funny."

Irma stared at him with a concerned expression on her face. "It certainly wasn't meant to be funny."

"Look, wait till you meet her, Irm, before you make up your mind. She's different. She's not that kind. She's something special."

"And you're not?"

"Not like her."

"Bull. Women would kill to warm your bed."

Jeremiah cut her a look. "Then why did I have to go on the auction block to get one?"

"Because you're too stubborn and pigheaded to let your friends fix you up with some nice young lady, that's why."

Jeremiah cursed. "Then what? She wouldn't want to live here, and I couldn't move where she was."

"Why not?"

"Because that ranch is mine, and I'll never leave it."

Irma blew out a breath. "Even though it's a struggle to make a go of it?"

"Even so," Jeremiah responded, his features grim. "I love every acre, and I intend to make a go of it. I'm determined to get my cattle to market if it kills me."

Irma reached out and patted his hand, a smile softening her face. "Don't get me wrong. I want you to make a success of your ranch, and I think you can. But more than anything, I want you to be happy again. But how is this woman different? Where is she from?"

"From Houston, actually. But, like me, she's searching for something, only I don't know what. Still, Bridget Martin can make me happy." Again his tone was belligerent; he silently admitted that he was trying to convince himself as well as Irma.

Irma smiled. "So tell me about this wonder woman."

He told her, leaving out, of course, the details of their passionate night of lovemaking. He couldn't quite come to terms with that in his own mind, much less try to explain it. He just knew that after he'd touched her on that dance floor and felt her nipples poke into his chest, he'd been a goner. He'd had to have her, and nothing short of death would have stopped him from taking what she had so freely offered.

"Have you told your aunt?"

"No, and I'm not going to. Not yet, anyway." Jeremiah held up his hand. "Bridget doesn't know about her, either."

"Do you honestly think this marriage has a chance of working?" Irma's tone was soft as concern clouded her eyes.

Jeremiah grabbed his hat and slapped it on his head. "One minute I'm sure of it, the next I'm not. I'm about as mixed up as I've ever been."

"I can understand that. It's not in your nature, Jeremiah Davis, to fly by the seat of your pants on anything."

He laughed, which made him feel better. "Well, there's always a first time for everything."

"So you think she'll still be there when you get home?"

A stabbing pain shot through him. "I have no idea. But speaking of home, I gotta go. I have a cow whose calf is going to be breech."

"In that case, maybe you'd best call Doc Minshew to help."

"Can't afford that old geezer. Besides, he's so blasted stubborn—"

Irma shook her head. "Now *that's* the pot calling the kettle black! You're more stubborn than any country vet I ever saw—country mule, either, for that matter."

Jeremiah laughed, then leaned over and pecked her on the cheek. "Don't ever change, Irma, love."

Blushing, she slapped him on the shoulder. "Go on, get out of here."

He had just reached his truck and was about to climb inside when Irma called out, "What about Taylor? Have you told your wife about—"

Jeremiah swung around, his gesture cutting her off. "No, I'm not ready for that yet, either."

Irma's false teeth clicked behind her tongue. "Seems to me you're asking for trouble all the way around."

"I want her to settle in as my wife first." Jeremiah heard the stubborn note in his tone and wanted to soften it, but he didn't know how. He felt vulnerable and afraid of himself and what he had done for the first time in his life. Still, he didn't intend for anyone else to know that, not even Irma, who he knew loved him like the son she'd never had.

After all, a man had his pride . . . or was supposed to.

"Tell her about Taylor, Jeremiah."

He nodded, then climbed into his truck and drove off. He didn't dare look back, for he knew Irma would be shaking her head in dismay again. And well she should.

Instead of thinking about Taylor, he was thinking that Bridget might have left. God forgive him.

Bridget heard his truck when it lumbered up the drive. She remained in the house, not wanting to face him. She had taken him at his word that he'd had to see to his herd, but apparently she'd been wrong to believe him. So where *had* he gone?

It didn't matter, she told herself when he didn't appear in the house. She didn't care. Besides, it was none of her business, she thought, only to realize that everything about this man was now her business.

He was her husband.

She couldn't dwell on that and keep her wits together, so she forced herself to do something. She ambled through the house, taking in the three bedrooms, tastefully but cheaply decorated. The living area sported fake leather furniture and a fireplace flanked by shelves filled with books and mementoes. It was only after she'd glanced through the memorabilia that she realized there were no pictures of his wife.

An eerie feeling passed through her when she asked herself how he'd continued to live here after his wife had died. More earth-shattering than that was the question of how he had made love to her in the same bed he'd shared with his wife.

Now, as she peered out the back window, Bridget asked herself that question once more, feeling sick inside. Their sleeping together didn't mean anything. Not to him. But it did to her, she told herself, especially the *way* they had made love. No man had ever touched her like Jeremiah had touched her.

Was that the real reason she had stayed?

A door slammed, and she flinched. But at least now she didn't have to answer that disturbing question. She heard voices from the front of the house. Moving to the door, she flung it open and stifled a cry. A television news van, with a major network's logo across the side in bold letters, was parked in front of the house.

"Oh, no," she whimpered behind the hand that covered her mouth, even as a cameraman was taping, while another man—an announcer, she decided, from the microphone clutched in his hand—walked toward the porch.

"Ma'am, are you Bridget Martin, the lady who participated in the auction?"

Mortified, Bridget stepped onto the porch. "Stop that camera right now."

"Why, ma'am? We're just doing our jobs. This is a hot story. You must know that."

"That's not the point. I don't—"

"What the hell's going on here?"

At the unexpected sound of Jeremiah's voice, Bridget whirled, then gasped. The Stetson was far back on his head, giving her a clear view of his face, which was twisted in fury. But what made her gasp was the blood that soaked the front of his shirt and jeans, as well as the towel he was wiping his hands on.

What had he been doing? she asked herself, trying to comprehend what was going on. He didn't look hurt.

"Can't you read, stud?" Jeremiah asked the news reporter.

"Of course, but—"

"Did you see the no trespassing sign on the gate?"

"Yes, but—"

"Forget the buts, mister. That sign is there for *your* health, not mine. So if you don't want to look like a squirming rat with that mike cord sticking outta your fanny, you'll get back in your little news wagon and hit the road."

Bridget left the porch and didn't stop until she reached Jeremiah's side. Her pulse was still racing from trying to figure out where all that blood had come from, not to mention the camera stuck in their faces.

As if he knew what she must be thinking, Jeremiah turned to her and muttered out of one side of his mouth, "A mama cow just had a breech birth."

"You can't stop us from doing our jobs!" the reporter screeched as the cameraman angled his camera closer.

Jeremiah thrust the lens aside. "You don't listen well, do you, friend?"

Before anyone could react, least of all the cameraman, Jeremiah gave him a hard push. The man landed square on his butt on the hard ground and rolled over, trying to protect the camera.

Jeremiah was on him immediately, deftly removing the camera from the man's grasp and pulling the film out of it. He waved it at the announcer.

"I'll bet you were too lazy to put in a fresh reel. This one probably has all the other bushwhack jobs you've done this mornin', right?"

There was an instant change in the men. Gone were the surly looks and hard-charging attitudes, replaced by wheedling and groveling.

"Now, Mr. Davis, we all have the same goal—"

"No, we don't. Your main goal right now had *better* be makin' it back to that van while those flashy teeth are still in your head. Your film stays with me, junior."

The cameraman scrambled to his feet, then, with his friend's help, gathered the equipment and shoved it into the van. Finally they got in themselves. It was then that Jeremiah noticed the second cameraman, who had remained inside, filming the entire incident.

"Damn!"

Once the announcer had the door safely locked behind him, he rolled down the window and shouted at Jeremiah, "You can keep that one, Davis. We have some *excellent* footage from our second camera."

His blood boiling, Jeremiah started toward the news van, but it spun out of the gravel drive, heading toward the cattle guard and the road beyond.

Once they had left the premises, Bridget stared at a tight-lipped Jeremiah, appalled at what had taken place, knowing that she had no choice but to call her parents.

"Well, I guess you know the balloon just went up," he said. "That film will be all over the national news by tonight."

"I know," she whispered, still staring at him. "Where'd you learn to handle a camera? You knew just how to take the film out."

"Oh, I worked for a TV station while I was in college."

"You went to college?" She knew she sounded incredulous.

"Sure. B.S. in animal husbandry. Why? Did you think I was stupid just because I took part in an auction?"

She didn't have an answer for that.

"So, are you hungry?" he asked.

She blinked. "Hungry?"

"Yeah, as in food." He smiled. "Do you people *eat* your cows in Texas, or do you just look at 'em?"

"That's not funny, and I'm not hungry."

"I am," he said in a flat tone. Then he angled his head. "So what's for dinner?"

At first it didn't dawn on Bridget what he was getting at. When it did, hot fury replaced her concern of a moment ago. Surely he didn't think she was going to feed him, for crying out loud? She gave him a hard look. No doubt about it, he was serious.

"Well?" he prodded.

She grinned, then quipped, "Lean Cuisine, what else?"

Nine

"So, where's your apron?" he asked.

Bridget looked up as Jeremiah sauntered into the living area from the shower, looking as good as he smelled, the faint odor of his musk cologne drifting to her. Although she knew he meant the question as a joke, she didn't think it was funny. Or maybe he *was* serious.

Either way, she didn't speak. His presence had robbed her of words. She was too caught up in the emotions he evoked in her. Her senses went haywire, which was not only ridiculous but infuriating. And frightening.

He watched her from the middle of the room, waiting for her answer, she knew. Still, she said nothing. He wore his white shirt outside his jeans; it wasn't buttoned all the way, allowing her to see the dark hair on his chest that contrasted with his tanned skin.

But he looked tired, as though he'd had a hard day. By all accounts he had, from delivering a baby calf—she flinched at the thought—to shoving a man down. Well, she was tired, as well, especially when she thought of how she'd behaved in his arms last night. Again, it struck her just how bizarre this entire situation was.

If she'd read this scenario in a book, or even if someone told her it had actually happened, she wouldn't have believed it. But it *had* happened. The fact that she was sitting here in this room, staring at the stranger who was her husband, was living proof.

How could she have married this man?

Jeremiah lifted his head, sniffed the air, then said into the silence, "Don't smell anything cooking, either."

"There's a good reason for that. It's because nothing *is* cooking." Her voice was sweet—too sweet.

He laughed, which again reminded her how much his animal attraction affected her.

"You *were* joking about the Lean Cuisine, right?"

She got up from the couch, but she kept her distance. She didn't want to get any closer to him than she already was. She didn't trust him, or maybe it was herself she didn't trust.

"Look, just so there's no confusion here, I never joke about my culinary skills, even if they *are* a joke. I don't know how to cook, and even if I did, I wouldn't do hard labor in *your* kitchen."

His smile fled, but when he spoke his tone was even, though there was a hint of an edge underneath the surface. "Well, I guess you'll just have to hone your skills in other ways."

"Such as?" she snapped.

He smiled again. "For starters, planting a garden and helping me with the chores on the ranch."

Bridget's eyes widened.

His narrowed. "You *can* ride a horse, can't you?"

"Of course I can't ride a horse."

He stiffened, then cursed, but never did he take his eyes off her.

Bridget sucked in her lower lip and gnawed on it, realizing that his gaze was stuck on her breasts. But then, he'd spent so much time nuzzling and sucking them last night that... Oh, dear Lord, she thought, panicked, reining in her thoughts. She couldn't keep thinking like that.

"I've never been on a horse in my life," she said in a frenzied tone.

"What about gardening?"

"Sorry, I don't know one end of a hoe from the other. And as a ranch hand, well—" She broke off and laughed without humor. "I'm a definite bust."

Jeremiah walked toward her. She wanted to back up, but her legs wouldn't allow it. They had all the consistency of wet noodles.

He kept on coming, his green eyes banked with suppressed fury. "You think all this is funny, don't you?"

"No, as a matter of fact, I think it's a tragedy," she retorted.

"I'd say it's turning into a nightmare."

"Which shouldn't come as any surprise."

"So I suppose that makes it all right, then," he sneered as he closed the distance between them. "Lets you off the hook, so to speak."

Bridget's chin jutted. She refused to let him know that his presence, along with his taunt, had increased her agitation.

"I never intended for this... farce to go this far," she said, licking her dry lips, while trying to hold on to her slipping composure. He was so close that she could see the fine lines around his eyes and mouth, lines that last night she had traced with her tongue. She felt the remaining color drain from her face, and it was all she could do to keep from groaning.

"Well, it's too late now." His smile was bitter. "You keep forgetting one small detail—you're my wife now, so this is no longer a farce."

"That can change."

"Like hell it can," he said, his tone sharp as a razor. "So what you're telling me is that you *can't* cook, you *can't* hoe and you *can't* ride a horse."

"Right. So you see, it's foolish for me to stay."

"Ah, but that's where you're wrong," he whispered, his minty breath cooling her skin. She stood rigid, especially when he ran a finger down one cheek.

That finger felt so possessive somehow, as if he was making his mark on her. Added to that, she was having difficulty fighting the crazy impulse to move against *him*.

"So tell me, is there anything you *are* good at . . . outside the bedroom, that is?"

She should have seen that coming, only she hadn't. Damn him! Bridget dug her nails into the palms of her hands during the electric silence that followed, aching to slap his insulting face. She didn't, but only because that was exactly what he wanted her to do.

Instead, her eyes flashed and her tone turned frigid. "You bastard. I'll tell you what I can do. I can try a civil lawsuit like a whiz. I can shop with the best Hollywood has to offer. And I'm proud that the only thing I make for dinner is reservations." She paused, letting what she'd said sink in. "So you see, there's no way this is going to work."

"Oh, but it will work," he said, reaching out and hauling her against him. "You want to know why?"

She struggled. "No, damn you, I don't."

"Yes, you do. Anyway, it's time you faced facts."

"*Me* face facts!"

"Yeah, you," he said, his tone dropping to a husky pitch at the same time that he slipped his hands down her arms and pinned them behind her. "Do you know how you make me feel? Like a randy teenager, hot and constantly hard."

"Jeremiah, please," she begged. "Stop this. You're acting like a kid, all right—a bully."

He eased his warm tongue inside her ear, and she whimpered, clutching at him.

"That's more like it," he whispered. "Remember last night how you begged me to touch you, to kiss you, to make *you* hot?"

"No!" she cried, desperate to prove him wrong. He made her sound like an insatiable hussy. She couldn't let him get away with that.

"Let me make love to you," he breathed against her lips, even as his hand snuck under her camp shirt and surrounded one breast.

A groan almost escaped her lips. Of all the days for her not to wear a bra.

His eyes flared, and she felt him harden against her stomach. "Stop!" she moaned.

"I can't."

"Yes, you can," she said, but her voice and her body were losing their willpower, especially as his mouth moved across hers. She was lost then and could deny him nothing. Feeling the room spin, she clung to him as his hard and hungry mouth stroked her lips apart. Her mouth opened, and her responsive body arched against him, aching to prolong the electric warring of their lips and tongues.

For a moment she gave in to her spinning senses, reveling in sensations reminiscent of last night, feeling his hand leave her breast and move to unfasten the top of her jeans.

It was that action that brought her to the bone-chilling reality of what she was doing, of what was actually happening. If she didn't call a halt to this madness now, they would be on the floor—or worse on the kitchen table—making love.

"Turn me loose!"

He let her go just as suddenly as he'd grabbed her. At first she was at a loss as to what to do without his arms around her; her entire body was weak and trembling. She sank her teeth into her lower lip and looked at him.

No doubt his body was in the same agony as hers. In spite of herself, her eyes dipped to the bulge beneath his zipper. He merely stared at her with contempt.

"This has got to stop," she said in a small voice. "I've already told you, everything can't be solved with sex."

"It'll sure go a long way in solving my problems, since it's obvious you're worthless at anything else."

"Go to hell!"

He grimaced. "I'm there, honey, right now. All you have to do is take another look at my zipper."

She flushed. "You're impossible. And I never looked at your zipper!"

"We both know that's a lie." He paused and drew a shuddering breath. "Okay, so I'm impossible... and lonesome, just like you."

That last statement came out of the blue. But its impact did as much to shake her as his aborted lovemaking. She stared at him, her mouth open.

He seemed reluctant to say anything else, and silence fell between them. Finally he said, "Look, we're married, and for whatever reason, you don't intend to bolt, at least not right now."

"I—"

"Don't interrupt. Let me finish. I've got good gut instincts, and right now my gut is telling me that you're hiding from something or running from someone. Or maybe both."

"What makes you think that?" she asked, fear shrinking her voice even more.

"I just told you, my gut instinct."

"I'm not guilty of either," she lied. "I have a home and parents who love me, I'll have you know." Only not in the way she longed to be loved, she thought with sadness. But he didn't have to know that.

"I guess the man in your life loves you, too."

"Of course."

He smirked. "Seems to me that if you'd had such a perfect life, you wouldn't be here. It just doesn't add up, sweetheart."

She saw red. One minute she ached to make love to him, and the next she ached to scratch his eyes out.

"I'm not your sweetheart," she said in a waspish tone.

"You're better. You're my wife."

She wilted, lacking an immediate comeback for that. Then she rallied and asked, "What about you?"

"What about me?"

She heard the leery note in his voice, which made her all the more curious, not that she hadn't been curious from the get-go. "Mother, daddy, brothers or sisters? Family is the word."

"My parents died when I was ten."

She gasped. "What happened?"

"My mother had cancer, and my dad had a stroke."

"So who took care of you?"

"An aunt and uncle, but my uncle's dead now." He paused. "When I graduated from high school, I left my aunt, did a stint in the service, then went to college and came back to the land my parents left me."

"And married your childhood sweetheart?"

His brows furrowed. "How'd you know?"

"Lucky guess." She paused and angled her head. "So tell me about your wife. What was she like?"

A look of misery crossed his face, and Bridget's heart sank.

"I'd rather not talk about her, if you don't mind."

"Fine. I looked around the house while you were gone."

"And?"

"I'm curious as to whose toys those are in one of the bedrooms." She knew he didn't have any children. If he had, he would have told her. Besides, a child was a living presence, not easily missed.

"They belong to a friend's kid," he said without looking at her.

"I see."

"Forget it," he said, his tone rough. "Like I said, if there was a woman in my life, why would I have resorted to such drastic measures as the auction?"

"I can't imagine."

A silence fell between them.

"So are you willing?" he asked.

"To do what?"

"Try and make this relationship work."

She didn't answer for the longest time, her thoughts in disarray. "There have to be some ground rules."

"Such as?"

"I won't share your bed."

"The hell you won't!"

Her voice rose to match his. "The hell I will!"

They glared at each other.

Finally he spoke. "Then you'd damned sure better figure out another way to make yourself useful."

Ten

He should have called the damn vet. If he had, maybe the calf would still be alive. But dammit, he hadn't been able to afford to send for the old rascal; that was the bottom line. He hated being in that position, but until he got his herd to market, he barely had two quarters to rub together.

And he had a wife to take care of.

A burning sensation began deep in Jeremiah's gut. Unable to ignore it, he fought the urge to kick the living daylights out of something. Instead, he reached for a piece of plastic and wrapped the calf in it. He had thought the heifer was going to make it. So much for his predictions.

He would have Willie Sampson take it down to the far pasture and bury it. Thank God for old Willie, Jeremiah thought, flexing his weary muscles. He was a longtime friend who was retired, with nothing to do except help him out around the ranch and sniff around Irma.

A smile tried to break through Jeremiah's gloom at the thought of that old coot chasing another old coot. Irma wasn't the least bit interested, or so she said. Jeremiah sometimes wondered if her protests weren't too blustering to be believable. But he didn't have time to worry about anyone else's love life, not with his own in the shape it was in.

Love life?

"Yeah right, Davis." His laughter was cynical, at best, as he trudged to the old sink and washed his hands. Gripping the edge of the cracked porcelain, he shut his eyes and drew a deep breath, only to find that pulling air through his lungs didn't calm him.

Last night had been disastrous. Hell, the whole day had been disastrous. Had Bridget Martin—he couldn't bring himself to add Davis to her name—been a part of his life for just two days? It seemed like much longer; then again, it didn't, which added to his confused state.

Cursing again, he slapped his wet hands against his jeans, then stalked outside, where the sunlight hit him. Too bad he wasn't in the mood to enjoy this perfect spring morning. But his mind wasn't on the weather—perfect or otherwise.

His thoughts were consumed with that dazzling, opinionated redhead inside the house who was the real reason for his foul mood this morning.

He hadn't slept any, either. Zilch. And he was bone weary. He couldn't do what he did around the ranch and not get his required hours of rest. But how the hell did one go about sleeping with a woman beside him who he ached to touch but wouldn't?

"Damn!"

Swearing didn't help any, either, especially when their heated conversation of the day before returned to the forefront of his mind.

He didn't know how long they had glared at each other before the volatile silence snapped.

"We've already made love, for heaven's sake!" he'd finally said.

"I wouldn't exactly call what went on between us making love." Her tone was scathing.

"Well, call it damn well anything you want to, but the bottom line is that we both needed it and enjoyed the hell out of it. If you deny that, then you're a liar."

"I don't lie."

"Good, then that's settled."

She shook her head. "No, it's not settled. If I stay, I won't sleep with you."

"You're my wife, Bridget. Wives sleep with their husbands."

"I—"

"You came here, remember? *You* bid on *me*. Maybe you were just a spoiled poor little rich girl on a lark, as you said. Or maybe, as I said yesterday, it was more." He held up his hand when she would have interrupted, but that didn't stop her.

"It was neither, damn you!"

"But it doesn't matter," he went on, "at least, not now. What matters is that you're here and that we're married." He paused. "And I need a wife in every sense of the word."

Silence followed his last bombshell, and while she was obviously confused and brooding, he used that silence to his advantage. "I'm going to do my chores. You think about what I said."

Well, she'd thought about it, because she'd slept beside him, though not with him. She had remained tense, as though she'd been strung on a rack. God! He couldn't break through that type of attitude, no matter how much he wanted her.

He'd looked at her, and, seeing her misery, he'd made up his mind. When he took her again, she would be warm and willing, aching as much as he was. In the meantime, he would have to bear it.

He had turned away from her and listened to the sounds of the night, his eyes wide open. When he'd crawled out of bed long before dawn, she'd been sleeping. He hadn't dare let his eyes linger on her, especially the creamy portion of one breast that was exposed.

He'd swallowed a curse, ignored his instant arousal, gotten up and dressed.

Now, as he rubbed his grainy eyes, he realized that nothing had been solved. What he ought to do was march inside the house and tell her to get the hell out. He might as well face the fact that she was no rancher's wife and never would be. So the thing to do was take the sucker punch he deserved and tell her to hit the highway.

Besides, their constant bickering was getting to him. As an attorney, she was used to jawing. He, on the other hand, coveted peace and tranquillity, something he'd had with Margaret.

But then, Margaret had never made his blood boil.

Suddenly realizing he was hungry, he stomped toward the house, praying for the strength to do what he knew he had to.

He heard her before he saw her. The instant he stepped on the back porch, her voice reached his ears. And whoever she was talking to, it wasn't making for a pleasant conversation.

He sighed, then opened the squeaky back door, a squeak that he'd been going to oil two months ago. He swallowed another curse and walked into the kitchen.

So as not to eavesdrop, he thought it best to let his presence be known.

When she heard him, she swung around, her eyes dark with anger. But this time, he knew that anger wasn't directed at him.

She turned around, then said, "I know you and Mother are upset, Daddy, but ya'll can't live my life for me any longer."

Jeremiah couldn't hear the man's response, but he could figure it out by Bridget's pursed lips and pinched face.

"I know Hamilton's upset, too, but I can't help that, either. So why don't we talk later, when we're both calmer?"

She listened a second longer, then hung up the receiver.

"So the boyfriend's upset, is he?"

"Don't start, Jeremiah."

"Well, Old Hamilton is just going to have to get used to the idea that you're married—and not to him."

He kicked himself mentally. So much for his good intention of waltzing in here and telling her that she was free to go—not that that choice hadn't been there all along. If she didn't want him, then he would damn well get over wanting her.

"Please don't start." Her tone sounded wobbly. "I can't take any more."

He sighed. "Neither can I." He paused. "They saw us on TV, huh?"

"That they did."

"Oh, boy."

"Needless to say, Anita and Allen are fed up with me."

"Does that bother you?"

She hesitated. "Yes, which I hate." Then, as if she realized she'd said too much, she shifted her gaze.

"Did you tell them?" he asked.

"That we were . . . married?"

He noticed she'd stumbled over the words, but let that go. Hell, he had trouble with those words, too. "Yeah."

"No. They couldn't handle that, not right now, anyway."

"But you are planning to tell them?"

She averted her gaze. "Sooner or later, I'll have to. But the fact that I . . . won you in an auction and that I'm living with you—" She broke off with a shiver, then added, "And to think they found out on TV."

Jeremiah's eyes darkened. "Thinking about those two jerks invading our privacy makes me sorry I didn't do more damage to them than I did."

"Oh, I think you got your message across."

He grinned. "Think so?"

"I know so."

They both laughed at the same time that their eyes met and locked.

"Er . . . where have you been?" she asked in a hurried tone, as if trying to put a stop to the sexual current running between them.

"In the barn," he responded, trying to fine tune his own tone. "The calf died."

"Oh, I'm sorry," she whispered.

He knew she was sincere, which made him feel somewhat better. There was another moment of awkward silence before he blurted out the first thing that came to mind. "Look, I need some supplies from town. Would you like to go and get them for me?"

Her face brightened. "I'd like that very much. I need to buy some things for myself and was wondering what I was going to do." When she had last spoken to Tiffany, her travel bag hadn't been mentioned.

Apparently, Tiff had carted it back home with her. It didn't matter; there had been very little in it.

"Well, if you're looking for the latest fashions in Pennington, you can forget it."

"I can buy a couple of pairs of jeans and shirts, can't I?" She paused. "And some personal things like..." Her voice faded into nothingness.

Panties and bras, he wanted to say, finishing the sentence for her. But he didn't voice the answer for fear of the repercussions. Anyway, as far as he was concerned, she didn't need either one.

"I think you can fill your basic needs," he said, wondering if she was wearing a bra now. She had on some damn shirt with pockets, so he couldn't tell.

He watched as she drew an uneven breath. "Good."

"But that's about it," he said, placing the conversation on even ground. "Pickings are real slim."

"No problem."

"You'll have to drive the pickup."

Her face fell.

He chuckled. "Don't worry. It's new, the only new thing around here."

"Well, in that case, I can handle it."

She smiled then, and for a second he fought the urge to grab her, kiss those delicious red lips and tongue that creamy breast he couldn't forget, which made him realize that the ache in his groin remained alive and well.

He cleared his throat. "When you hop into town, go to Irma's Place and ask for Irma herself. She's a neat old broad. You'll like her."

"Neat old broad, huh?" She smiled. "Whatever you say."

He reached in his pocket and tossed her the keys. "Be careful, okay?"

She nodded, then licked her lips. He groaned.

"Okay," she said, her voice barely audible.

When she reached the door, he stopped her. "Anything special you want for dinner?"

"Do you think I'm less of a woman because I can't cook?"

That question was so unexpected that he was too stunned to answer. To make matters worse, he heard the uncertainty in her voice, which made him crazy to hold her. Instead, he put the brakes on his desire to show her that nothing she did or didn't do would ever make her less of a woman in his eyes. But all he could do was stand there and run his hot gaze over her luscious body. When he spoke, his voice was gentler than it had ever been.

"No way, honey. You're more of a woman than even you realize."

She stared at him for a moment longer, then turned and practically ran out of the house. Only after he heard the engine start did he cross to the cabinet, grab a skillet and slam it on a burner.

"One of these days, Davis, you're gonna learn to keep your mouth shut!"

Grrupp. The deep, mournful protest from the transmission as Bridget searched for the gear caused Jeremiah to wince; it was like fingernails across a chalkboard to his ears. Grrupp. Twice more he clenched his teeth, determined to ignore it. One particularly majestic clash of gears, lasting a full ten seconds, sent him over to the window to check on her. He would bet Bridget had never driven a standard shift in her life!

His green pickup hopped across the front yard, looking for all the world like the Celebrated Jumping Frog of Calaveras County. Hell, he would need a new clutch in another few minutes.

Jeremiah raced out the door and across the drive, but he was too late. After a few more grrupps and two wildly majestic leaps, his pickup was disappearing down the road. He kicked the dirt with his boot. Was there *anything* that woman could do right?

Out here, stick shifts were everywhere. Kids learned to drive on them, and it had never entered his mind, prior to Bridget's crazed exhibition of incompetence, that she wouldn't know how to handle one. There was a seventy percent chance his truck would come home swinging from the back of a wrecker. After all, the whole drive train couldn't be hanging by more than one bolt by now!

"Damn!"

Then, in spite of himself, he chuckled. Even if it cost him a new clutch or even a transmission, he wouldn't change a single second of watching—and listening to—that beautiful woman "hop into town."

Eleven

———

Bridget laughed as she stared at the tiny woman with skin the color and texture of the saddles she sold in her store.

"You should laugh more often, my dear," Irma said, tilting her head to one side and staring at Bridget.

Bridget sobered. "I know, only I haven't had a lot to smile about lately."

"So you regret marrying Jeremiah?"

Once again Bridget was taken aback by Irma's directness, though she should have adapted to the old woman's ways by now. She'd been sitting in Irma's tiny living room at the back of her store sipping coffee and nibbling on a slice of her fresh baked wheat bread for over thirty minutes, enjoying every moment. She'd liked the old woman on sight, even though Irma hadn't minced words from the get-go. However, until now, she'd never commented on Bridget and Jeremiah's unorthodox marriage.

"Well, you'll have to admit that most marriages don't start out under such weird circumstances," Bridget responded, bridging the silence.

Irma wrinkled her nose, then batted her hand. "The important thing here is that both of you make up your mind that you want it to work, then do it."

Bridget's head jerked. "Do you really think that's possible?"

"'Course it's possible, child. Anything's possible if you want it bad enough."

"You care a great deal about Jeremiah, don't you?" Bridget's tone was soft.

"He's the son I never had, and he's been dealt far too many blows in his life already, more than anyone should have to bear."

So in other words, Bridget, don't bring him any more grief, she translated, before saying, "You're referring to the loss of his wife, right?"

"That's just one of many blows. His raising was unfit, and he's had rotten luck with his cattle."

"Nothing seems to get him down."

"That's because he'll do for others before he'll do for himself, though he's always been a loner."

"Those two traits seem like they'd be on opposite ends of the spectrum."

Irma sighed. "After Margaret died, he withdrew into a shell and worked, worked, worked."

"What about his aunt? Does he go see her?"

Irma seemed to hesitate. "Every week, sometimes twice. They have a good relationship, but—" She stopped midsentence.

"But what?" Bridget prodded, hoping Irma would shed more light on Jeremiah and his family, which included his deceased wife. But she didn't want to ask; she would rather have Irma volunteer the information.

"But nothing," Irma said, looking away, "except that I've talked too much." She grinned. "But then, that's my downfall. I like you, Bridget Davis."

Bridget smiled, though the name "Davis" attached to hers gave her a moment's start. "And I like you, Irma Quill."

"So are you going to stay?"

"As in married to Jeremiah?"

"Yes."

"I don't know, Irma. Right now, I can't see us together. Yet there's something about him that's—" This time Bridget broke off, groping for words that wouldn't come.

"I know." Irma's usual abrupt tone had mellowed. "You don't have to explain or apologize. That's what makes him special."

Twenty minutes later, as Bridget traveled the lonely highway toward the ranch, those words kept bouncing around in her brain. He *was* special, so special that all he had to do was walk into the same room with her and she wanted him to touch her, which kept both her heart and her mind in a tizzy.

She had purchased the clothes and personal items she'd gone after, as well as the supplies Jeremiah had wanted. But she didn't know if she would be there long enough to use her things. With that thought weighing on her, she focused on the view.

This part of the country was so different from Texas. Yet the simple life here both amazed and calmed her. She'd even noticed how much her anxiety had lessened. Maybe if she hung around, she could toss her pills away forever.

"You're dreaming," she mused aloud, her features turning bitter for a moment.

No way could she ever adapt to the loneliness, the inconveniences, the weather or the sheer distances be-

tween places in this part of the world. She needed
people and bright lights to survive. She'd been lonely
all her life, and she didn't want any more of it. However, getting out of this situation was another matter
altogether. It wouldn't be easy.

More disturbing was the fact that she wasn't in any
hurry to leave, despite the misery of last night when
she'd shared his bed—if not his arms—which had been
one of the hardest things she'd ever done. Maybe she
enjoyed being a masochist.

When she pulled into the drive a short time later,
Jeremiah was rounding the corner of the house. For a
moment Bridget was certain his features brightened
when he saw her. She felt a catch in her heartbeat, for
sure. She wished she knew what there was about him
that always caused that hot, aching feeling between her
legs.

But when he charged toward the truck and jerked
open the door, that warmth disappeared.

"Where the hell have you been?"

"I'm doing fine, Mr. Davis, and you?" Bridget responded in an icy voice. "Besides, you know damn
well where I've been."

"Well, you've been gone a hell of a long time."

Bridget scrambled out of the truck. "So what? I like
Irma, and her wheat bread is great."

"Is that all you've got to say?"

"Yes, so get out of my way and leave me alone."

With that she dashed toward the house, feeling his
smoldering eyes tracking her every step.

Why the hell didn't she just go back where she belonged?

During the following week that question haunted
Bridget because nothing went right. She tried to ride
a horse; she fell off and bruised her butt. She tried to

hoe the garden, only to get a handful of blisters. She
experimented in the kitchen, only to almost burn it
down.

Jeremiah's attitude added fuel to an already raging
fire inside her. His lips had twitched at the horse incident. He'd bought her gloves for gardening. But
when she'd sent smoke billowing to the kitchen ceiling, he'd lost it.

"Dammit, woman!"

"Don't you dare yell at me!" she'd countered. "At
least I'm trying."

"Not hard enough. You're a walking disaster!"

While that last remark had indeed added to her fury,
it paled in comparison to the nights. They were the
worst. She lay beside him on her side of the bed, so far
away that at times she feared she might fall off. Yet he
never touched her, which had her nerves screaming.

Finally, two nights ago, he'd propped himself up on
an elbow and stared at her in the moonlight. "Look,
this can't go on for either one of us, so why don't you
just chill, okay?"

"Me?" Her voice sounded as if it came from
someone else. "What about you?"

"I'm not about to force myself on you."

"You did once."

"That's a damned lie. You wanted me inside you
that night as badly as I wanted to be there. But don't
worry. It's not going to happen again."

She sat up in the bed. "You're right, because I'm
moving into one of the other bedrooms. Now!"

And she had been true to her word. She was sleeping alone in another bedroom. At best an uneasy truce
had been established, though she had no idea how
much longer it would last, especially given the heightened tension between them. One or both of them
would be sure to snap. She could hear his movements

during the night; only a wall separated her head from his.

So why didn't she just end this farce and return home? She didn't want to; it was that simple. Nothing had changed in Houston—no job; fake friends, Tiffany being the only exception; parents who were too self-involved to care about her, unless it was in their interest to do so. A sadness settled inside her, and she gave in to it, feeling the threat of tears.

Yet her life was in Texas. She couldn't hide forever. And she *was* capable of starting over. So why didn't she? It was time she stopped playing games with herself, time she acted like the intelligent realist she'd always been.

She didn't want to leave Jeremiah Davis. That was the unvarnished truth. She didn't love him, could never love him, but she wanted him. And until she assuaged the ache inside her, she couldn't leave, no matter how much she might want to.

Okay, she'd admitted that, which should have made her feel better. So why didn't it?

"Grow up, Bridget, for heaven's sake!" she muttered while stirring a bowl of uneaten cereal.

It was then that the phone rang. Flinching, she stared at it for the longest time, expecting Jeremiah to answer it, then remembered that he was in the barn.

Sighing, she got up, walked to the buffet and lifted the receiver.

"Hello?"

It was a man asking for her, but Bridget didn't recognize the voice. "Speaking."

"I'm Wayne Parker, an attorney in Houston."

Bridget's grip on the phone tightened. "As in Parker, Hughes and Lambert?"

He chuckled, as though he picked up on the awe in her tone. "One and the same."

Bridget cleared her throat. "I'm pleased to meet you, Mr. Parker, even if it is only on the phone."

"Well, maybe we can solve that little technical matter."

"How's that?" Bridget shook all over. Why was he calling her? She knew he was a good friend of her father's, but still . . .

"We have an opening in our Houston litigation section, and the job's yours if you want it."

Bridget's mouth gaped. "Just like that?"

"Just like that."

"Did my dad put you up to this, because if he did—"

"Whoa, Miss Martin. Allen's my friend, all right, but he doesn't have any say-so in who we hire for this firm."

"So why me, then?" Her tone was suspicious.

"Because you're a damned good attorney, and that's what we're looking for."

"You know about the sexual harassment suit I filed?" She didn't see the need to be anything less than candid. Doing so now would save her time, disappointment and heartbreak.

"I know, but that has nothing to do with us. That's your business. So, are you interested?"

"Very."

"Good, then when can we talk in person?"

"What does the job involve?"

"Trying court cases, pure and simple. It's litigation, civil defense. Mostly toxic torts, though we do have several other things coming up soon."

Bridget's excitement took another leap. Oh, Lord, that was what she wanted, but could she do it? At the moment, she felt she could. Nothing akin to panic washed through her. Still, she didn't want to make a hasty decision.

"I'm definitely interested, but I need time to think about it."

"Well, you can have a week."

"Is that all?"

"That's all, I'm afraid. We need that position filled ASAP."

"Thanks for your confidence. I'll certainly give your offer serious thought. It's been nice talking to you, Mr. Parker." She hung up, a thoughtful expression on her face.

"Who's Mr. Parker?"

She hadn't heard Jeremiah come in, and her heart dropped to her toes. "You scared me," she whispered, turning around.

"Sorry. Didn't mean to."

She swallowed, thinking he looked like hell—hot and sweaty and exhausted. But even those minuses didn't stop her knees from knocking, and it wasn't because he'd frightened her, either. If he'd yanked her into his arms, she wouldn't have stopped him. Mortified at her thoughts, she stared at her feet.

"So who's Mr. Parker?"

"An attorney in Houston."

"What did he want?"

"He offered me a job."

"I see."

Silence.

"So are you going to take it?"

"I—"

The phone rang again.

"Damn!" Jeremiah said, his eyes clinging to her, but he made no effort to move.

She forced herself to ask, "Aren't . . . you going to answer it?"

"Do you want me to?"

She swallowed hard. "Yes."

"Damn," he muttered again, before reaching for the receiver.

Bridget watched as his face turned white. "I'll be right there!"

"What's the matter?" she asked, her mouth dry, sensing it was bad news.

"Gotta go. John Henry's house is on fire, and the fire's threatening to spread."

"I'm coming with you," she said, following him out the door.

He stopped and swung around. "No, you're not. You'd just be in the way."

His remark hurt, but she jutted out her chin and said, "No, I won't. Besides, you can't tell me what to do." She dashed to the truck and climbed inside.

"Women!" He got in beside her, slammed the door, cranked the engine, then spun toward the neighboring ranch.

Twelve

Jeremiah had never felt so helpless in his life, except when his wife had died. Thank God the three years since that tragedy had healed him, and he'd been able to go on with his life, bleak though it had been.

But when he'd first driven to this ranch three days ago and looked at what remained of the charred house, he'd experienced that familiar sick feeling inside.

Miracles do happen, he told himself as he peered at the structure that was fast shaping into a new home. It hadn't been easy. By the time he and Bridget had arrived on the scene, the house had been a goner. Still, the danger hadn't ended; the uncontained fire remained a threat. It had taken the remainder of the day to trap the flames before they consumed the nearby pastureland.

The experience had been harrowing and dangerous, one he would never forget, nor would Bridget, he knew, though little had been said between them that first night following the fire.

"Do you want me to doctor your hands?" she'd asked in a hesitant tone when they had gotten back to his ranch.

Surprised that she would even suggest such a thing, he swung around. That was when he realized how close she was to him. Alarm flickered in his veins as her lips parted, giving him a tantalizing glimpse of her tongue.

His blood pressure rose, and it was all he could do not to touch her. "Forget my hands," he said, his voice low and husky. "There's another part of my body that needs doctoring a hell of a lot more."

He saw the alarm jump into her eyes at the same time that she stepped back as though she'd been singed, and not by the fire, either. "I...can't," she whispered.

"Can't—or won't?"

"I need more time."

"That's one thing we don't have. The sound I hear in the background is a clock ticking."

Jeremiah gave his head a sudden, violent shake, his thoughts returning to the present. He'd had no intention of rehashing that scene. Somehow, it had snuck up on him.

"Hey, Davis, get the lead out of your butt and let's get started," a fellow worker called out.

Making the most of the interruption in his thoughts, Jeremiah drew an uneven breath, then let it out. "Hold your horses. I'm coming."

Yet he found it difficult to get his mind on track, especially when Bridget was there, strutting around in those tight jeans.

His eyes zeroed in on her, and he watched as she chased after one of the many children who were there with their parents. She seemed to have a knack with the kids, though she would probably deny that. Maybe he should tell her— Hell, what was he thinking? To spill his guts now would be suicidal and useless.

She wasn't going to be around much longer, anyway. But while she was here, he was going to make the most of looking at her. He liked her tight rear end, the way the sunlight bounced off her hair, making it look like a burning bush. Actually, he liked everything about her. Yet he could never have her.

She'd told him the truth when she'd admitted that she was useless as a rancher's wife. In her world, he had no doubt that she was both efficient and resourceful. But what had caught him off guard was that feminine streak that made him want to protect her from the harshness of this life.

Hell, he'd never felt that way about Margaret, though he'd certainly felt protective of her in other ways. But Bridget was different. She was a mixture that baffled him, arousing new impulses in him, which continued to work on his nervous system.

What scared him the most, though, was wondering how much longer he could resist the temptation to just walk into her room at night and take her into his arms.

And to hell with the consequences.

"Hell, Davis, you think you're on vacation or something?"

At the sound of a fellow worker's coarse voice, he jumped again. "Sorry."

"No need to be sorry. Just get your butt back to work."

Jeremiah forced a grin, got up and picked up his hammer, careful not to let his eyes stray to Bridget.

"Well, I'm sure this makes you wish you were back in civilization, doesn't it?"

Bridget looked at a weary-faced Irma and smiled. "Actually, no."

Irma's head jerked. "You're pulling my leg."

"No, truly, I'm not. While I must look like a misplaced modifier, I don't feel like one."

Irma slung an arm across Bridget's shoulders and squeezed. "If it's any consolation, you don't look like one, either. In fact, you've been a real trooper throughout this terrible ordeal."

"I haven't done anything, though I've tried."

"Huh, you've done as much as any of us."

"I haven't, but it makes me feel good to hear you say that."

Bridget knew she would never hear that praise from Jeremiah, even though his opinion was the one that counted. Still, she warmed to Irma's praise now, just as she had to the other women's earlier. They, too, had complimented her on her attempts to help, though her most heroic efforts had been watching the children while the women cooked and helped the men with the carpentry work.

"Instead of knocking yourself, you should be patting yourself on the back," Irma was saying with a grin. "You've come a long way, honey."

Bridget frowned. "I can't deny that, though I made a fool of myself in the process."

"Don't you dare say that. Believe me, I wasn't born knowing what a two-by-four was."

"You might not have known what a two-by-four was, but you sure could've gotten a bucket of nails up a ladder."

Irma chuckled. "It was an accident. Forget it. Look, I'm about to leave, okay? I have to get back to the store—see to my own business, especially now that the house is about finished."

"I suspect Jeremiah'll want to be leaving soon, too," Bridget responded, her eyes tracking him.

"Yep, I'm sure he will. So I'll see you later."

"I hope so."

Once Irma left, Bridget's thoughts returned to the woman's words of praise. Maybe she *was* being too hard on herself. After all, Susan Henry had also told her how much she appreciated all she'd done. That was when Bridget realized that she'd established a rapport with these women, some who had taken part in the auction and some who had lived here already.

The thing that had made the strongest impression on her during her time here was the camaraderie that these people in the community shared, the willingness to drop what they were doing and help someone in need. Jeremiah, in particular, was concerned for everyone's well-being.

If only she hadn't made a fool of herself yesterday when she'd gotten her first taste of manual labor. She didn't care what Irma had said—she felt awful.

The men had asked for a bucket of nails. Looking around, she found that she'd been the only woman available, so she had volunteered. She'd scooped the nails out of the bag with her bare hands until the bucket was full. Only after she'd tried to carry it did she realize it was too heavy. Yet she'd been determined to help them.

She'd lugged the bucket, all the while wincing as it banged against her legs. It was after she'd stepped on the first rung of the ladder and tried to lift the container to Jeremiah that disaster had struck. Her foot slipped. Both she and the bucket took a tumble.

Jeremiah had practically jumped off the ladder to get to her. "Are you okay?" he'd demanded, kneeling beside her.

"Yes," she said, mortified, then scrambled to get up.

"Hey, Davis!" a man on the roof hollered. "Seems like you got your work cut out for you!"

Jeremiah threw the man a dirty look.

"Ah, don't get riled," the man responded. "I was just teasing. Your little lady's doing a fine job."

She hadn't done a fine job, and they both knew it. It wasn't discussed, however. On the way home, she hadn't said anything, still smarting. She'd sat beside him like a statue.

Later, after she'd fallen into bed, so tired that every muscle in her body felt stretched to the breaking point, she hadn't felt any better. She'd told herself it was because she kept playing that embarrassing incident over in her mind, but she knew better.

Her restlessness had stemmed from the fact that he was in the room next to hers. Every time he moved, which was often, she'd heard him. He had seemed as restless as she was, and she couldn't help but wonder if he was having as much of a problem combating his passion for her as she was fighting hers for him.

Now, as she watched Jeremiah, high on the roof, shirtless, sweat pouring off his body, she experienced another surge of heat through her body. That heat flourished as he climbed off the roof and headed toward her. "You ready to go home?" he asked, reaching for his Stetson where it sat on a picnic table and slapping it on his head.

Home. That word again.

"I think it's time, don't you? Anyway, it's getting dark," he added.

A short time later, they made their way into the house. It hurt to walk, and she was slow getting up the front steps.

"Ouch!" she muttered to herself, managing to make it into the living room.

"Are you hurt?" Jeremiah asked.

"No, it's nothing, really. When I fell, I must've pulled a muscle." Damn, couldn't she do anything right?

"I noticed your hands were banged up, too," he said, his eyes narrowing.

"It's okay. Really. You're the one who's banged up. You look like you're about to drop in your tracks."

"I'm okay."

"No, you're not."

"Hey, you're beginning to sound like a wife." He paused, and when he spoke again, his voice was like gravel. "Only we both know you're not."

They stared at each other in stony silence.

Bridget shifted her feet, feeling a lump form in her throat. She cleared it. "Look, now's not the time for this." She paused. "You should go to bed."

"And you should go home."

Bridget blinked. "Excuse me?"

"You heard what I said."

"I am home."

His laugh was sinister. "No, you're not, not by a long shot."

"You mean home as in Houston?" She looked at him with disbelief.

"That's exactly what I mean." His tone was harsh and unyielding.

"But—" She shook her head, perplexed.

He reached for her hands, stared at them, then looked at her face, his features twisted. "It's obvious this isn't the life for you. So just get the hell back where you belong."

The panic building in her stomach suddenly exploded. "You wait just one minute! I'm not ready to leave, but when I am, it'll be on my terms."

"Well, if you stay," Jeremiah cautioned, "it'll be on *my* terms."

"And just what are those?"

His eyes dipped to her chest, where her breasts heaved from her outburst of temper, then returned to her flushed face.

"You in my bed, with me inside you."

Thirteen

His lips, hot and seeking, searched for hers, beginning at her ear and working across her cheek. Even though his mouth was making her weak all over, she held back, stiffening in his arms.

"Don't, please." Her plea came in a broken, tormented voice.

"I have to. What are you trying to do to me—drive me out of my mind?" Then his mouth found hers with unerring accuracy, hotter and more determined than ever, his tongue licking her lips apart.

"This...we shouldn't," she whispered in agony, their breaths mingling. "It's...crazy.... It's..."

"Please, I need you. You can feel how much."

"You need *sex*," she responded, her voice broken.

"Why do you fight this—fight *me?* You know this is what we both want, what we both *need*."

"I have to...fight you." But she couldn't, and he knew it. Her voice held no conviction and no will to resist him; he'd robbed her of that already with his lips and with his maleness throbbing against her thigh.

His mouth landed on hers again, hard and possessive, while he lifted her into his arms and carried her to the bed. She trembled all over, yet she could hardly stand to be parted from him while he discarded his clothes, then removed hers.

His eyes were lazy as they roved over her. "You're almost too beautiful to touch. I'm afraid—"

"Shh." She didn't want to talk. Talking might bring a return to sanity and spoil the moment. She wanted to kiss and be kissed, and to feel that hot urgent flow of electricity between them.

"I understand," he whispered.

A sob rose in her throat when his hands began exploring her body, rubbing against her before he eased a finger inside her moistness.

"Jeremiah—Jeremiah, please . . ."

She hadn't meant to give in to this madness again. But her whole body was on fire, burning for him. She had to have him; she couldn't settle for less, having never met a man whose hands and lips had the power to mold her, to manipulate her, until nothing else mattered except him.

"I'm hurting, too, baby. I can't wait much longer."

She knew that was true, because her hands weren't idle. They had moved down his back, over his buttocks, exploring with excitement and heat.

"You little minx," he groaned; then, bending over, he circled a nipple with his lips at the same time that he buried himself deep inside her. She clutched his back with nerveless fingers and wound her legs around him.

Despite her plea, he seemed determined to hold back, to build her desire to an even higher pitch.

"Jeremiah!"

He thrust again, and she cried out along with him.

Then a feverish hunger claimed them both, and only after the longest time was that hunger satisfied, ending in an exhausted sleep.

When Bridget awoke to blinding sunlight streaming through the window, she noticed Jeremiah wasn't beside her. She groaned, realizing she'd done exactly what she'd said she wouldn't do again. She wouldn't think about that now, though.

Moving gingerly, she reached for her panties and shirt, slipped into them, then made her way toward the bathroom. She opened the door, and her mouth fell open. "Oh!" she cried, feeling her face turn crimson.

Jeremiah was standing naked in front of the mirror, shaving.

"Morning," he said, continuing with what he was doing.

"Uh ... sorry."

He laughed. "Come on in."

"That's all right." Her tongue was thick. "I'll wait."

He faced her. "You're embarrassed, aren't you?"

When she didn't say anything, his laughter deepened. "Don't you think it's a bit late for that sorta thing?"

"It's not funny," she said, though she didn't shift her gaze.

"Sure it is." Jeremiah paused, then out of the blue asked, "Would you like to saddle up and learn how to ride?"

"Now?"

"Yep. Why not? It's a beautiful morning."

"Okay," she said, then wondered when she was going to start thinking with her head instead of her heart.

A short time later, at the barn, he laughed as she stood in front of what seemed like the biggest horse she'd ever seen. "He won't hurt you, I promise."

Bridget eyed the horse with suspicion. "Why isn't he a she?"

Jeremiah rolled his eyes heavenward as though praying for divine guidance.

Bridget giggled, yet her laughter was rooted in nerves rather than merriment. "I just figured I might get along better with another woman. He... he looks so big and intimidating."

"He's big, all right, but a she would be just as big." Jeremiah grinned, then leaned over and gave her a hard, wet kiss. "Mmm, good. If you don't quit stalling, Mrs. Davis, we can forget this riding lesson."

"And do what?" she teased, though with a catch in her voice.

His gaze smoldered. "Throw you down on the ground so I can have my way with you."

By the time he'd spoken those antiquated words, he was grinning from ear to ear.

Bridget lifted her chin in the air. "I'm sorry, you'll just have to control your libido for a little while longer."

He kissed her again, then pulled away, far away. "You're right. I've already taught you how to ride me—"

She stared at him, aghast.

He laughed. "Well, it's the truth. So now I have to teach you how to ride a horse."

"You're impossible," she responded with a breathless tremor in her voice. But she ate it up; in fact she ate *him* up, which made her heart skip another beat. Where was all this leading? She still couldn't believe they had any kind of future together. Yet...

"Come on, stop woolgathering and saddle up."

"How . . . I mean . . ."

Again he rolled his eyes. "Why, sweetheart, you just swing that cute little butt of yours into the saddle."

She glared at him. "I know that, only it's not that simple."

"Sure it is. But come on, I'll give you a push. Anything to get my hands on those buns of yours."

Grinning, she slapped his hands even as they cupped the cheeks of her buttocks. "Oh, no, you don't. Since you've opened your big mouth, I'll show you that I can mount a horse."

His lips curved into a knowing smile, then he leaned over and whispered, "If you can mount him like you mount me, you won't have a problem."

"Is that all you think about?" Bridget retaliated, but without much vigor. His sexual innuendoes were driving her wild, making her ache for him again. But how could she? They had made love throughout the night, with both sweet and savage intensity, until she was sore, too sore to be trying to learn to ride a horse.

However, she wanted to be with him, to please him in every way, knowing even as she thought such a thing that she was asking for trouble. He didn't love her, nor did she love him. They just had an insatiable appetite for one another, that would disintegrate in time. As she'd already told him, sex alone was not enough to bond two people together for a lifetime.

Lifetime.

Now, that had a ring to it that she liked. Yet she knew it wasn't possible. They were from two different worlds, and at the moment she didn't see how those two worlds could merge into one and let both of them be happy. Granted, she was happy now, basking in the sexual pleasures he brought to her and she to him, but it really was only temporary.

"Stop stalling, will you?"

She turned and saw that his back was to her. Either he was fooling with his saddle on purpose to give her time to mount by herself, or something was wrong. She suspected her first thought was the correct one.

"How did you know I hadn't mounted? Don't tell me you have eyes in the back of your head."

Jeremiah swung around and chuckled. "Don't have to. Believe me, you won't climb atop old Mackie without making noise. So, are you ready?"

She eyed Mackie, who appeared as docile as a newborn puppy, only she knew better.

"Sure you don't want my help?"

"No," she said with far more conviction than she was feeling. Her stomach revolted. "I'm a big girl. Hell, I'm an attorney. I'll just pretend this big lug here is the plaintiff's lawyer in Houston and I'm eager to kick his butt all over the courtroom."

Jeremiah pitched back his head and laughed. "Atta girl. Give old Mackie hell. Show 'em who's boss."

It was only after she'd clamped her hand onto the saddle horn and placed her boot in the stirrup that a gunshot blasted through the quiet morning air, sounding like a sonic boom.

Jeremiah jerked his head toward the mountains. "What the hell?"

Bridget's heart landed around her feet as Mackie flinched, then perked his ears. She was about to remove her boot from the stirrup when he took off running.

"Oh, my God!" she cried as he pulled her with him.

"Bridget! Let go!"

She heard Jeremiah's harsh command, but she couldn't have let go if her life depended on it, even though, at that moment, she felt sure that it did. It was as if her hand was glued to the saddle horn.

"Turn loose!" Jeremiah hollered again. "I'm coming!"

Maybe it was that assurance that gave her the strength to do what Jeremiah demanded of her. Still, she hesitated, fear surging though her body with the same force and speed that Mackie was dragging her. What if the impact with the ground broke every bone in her body?

"Oh, my God, oh, my God, oh, my God!" she cried again.

"Just do it!"

She did it. She let go, then hit the ground with a thud and lay unmoving as stars shot through her brain.

"Are you all right? Bridget! Answer me!"

She heard Jeremiah's aching cry, but she didn't have the strength or the wherewithal to say a word. Yet she was alive. She knew that much; she could see him leaning over her. Moaning, she tried to move.

"Don't. Hold still. Let me see if anything's broken."

She did as she was told and felt his hands move all over her. He was asking questions as he went along. "Does this hurt? Can you move this?"

"Yes and yes."

"It appears you don't have any broken bones. God, you scared the living daylights out of me."

Now that she'd gotten her breath, she asked, "What . . . happened?"

"Some idiot was probably target shooting, which I don't allow on my property. If I could get my hands on him, I'd tear him limb from limb."

"It's okay. I'm all right, though I don't think I'll learn to ride today."

With his face pale and his hand unsteady, Jeremiah touched the side of her face. "If anything had happened to you—'' He broke off and looked away for a second, as though trying to get hold of himself.

"It didn't. That is, nothing serious. I'm just winded, and my pride's hurt, of course."

"Forget pride. I'm just glad you didn't break your neck. If only I hadn't insisted you learn to ride."

"Hey, I wanted to learn, and I still do." She smiled, adding, "Only not today."

He chuckled, which relieved some of the strain from his face. "You sure about that?"

"I'm sure. So, are you going to get off me?"

"No."

The atmosphere turned thick and heavy.

"What does that mean?"

"It means that I'm going to do what I've wanted to do ever since we came out here."

Jeremiah's hand moved between her thighs, gently, as he'd done when checking for broken bones. "Is anything broken here?"

Bridget pushed herself up to meet him, then ground herself into his hand.

"I don't think so," she said, her breath coming in ragged snatches.

"Good. I don't want to hurt you."

She looped her arms around his neck, drew his head down and whispered, "You won't hear any complaints from me."

Fourteen

"Jeremiah," she groaned. "Jeremiah?"

"It's okay, I'll be easy."

"Don't."

He chuckled, his mouth close to hers. "After all, you just took a hard tumble."

"Not that hard." She peered at him through glazed eyes—though not from the fall. Oh, she knew she would be sore tomorrow, but nothing was hurt except her pride, which in the scheme of things no longer mattered. All that mattered was having Jeremiah inside her. Again.

"I've never made love outdoors before," he whispered, all the while unbuckling her belt, her jeans, then sliding them past her knees to her ankles.

"Not even with your...wife?" Bridget hadn't planned to ask that. The words had just slipped past her lips.

He didn't seem to take offense. Still, a strange, un-identifiable look crossed his face. "She wasn't the type."

Bridget felt vaguely offended, yet she didn't stop him from unzipping his jeans and watched avidly as he released his aroused sex. She swallowed before forcing herself to look at him. "What does that mean?"

"Do we have to talk about this now?" His voice sounded pained.

"Yes."

He rubbed his hand over her stomach, which took her breath for a moment. The effect this man had on her...

"What I meant to say was that she didn't particularly like sex."

"But you loved her?" Bridget hated asking that question, especially now, yet for some perverse reason, she had to know.

He hesitated while a faraway look changed his eyes. "Yes, I loved her, but I wasn't ever passionately in love with her. There's a difference, you know." He leaned down and kissed Bridget with fierce intensity. "Enough talking, all right?"

How could it not be all right, especially with his lashing tongue in her mouth and his hand cupping her between her thighs where she ached?

She raised her hips to get closer to him, but the constriction of the clothes around her ankles was proving to be a problem, at least for her. But apparently not for him, for his callused hands had no difficulty in spreading her thighs. Still feeling constricted, she shifted to her side, kicking free of the jeans.

Then he rolled her over to face him. Her eyes fluttered. "What—"

He clasped her tighter, then thrust inside her. Her mouth parted, and she gasped even as she felt all of him. Her hands latched onto his shirt as they crashed and melted together.

Only the animals heard their moans.

Afterward Jeremiah looked at her for the longest time, smoothing the moist hair from her forehead.

"Are you okay?"

She smiled. "I'm fine."

"I bet you won't say that tomorrow."

"I'll deal with that when it comes."

He was silent for a moment, as if trying to find the courage to spit out what was on his mind. "What about that job?"

She held her breath. "What about it?"

"Are you going to take it?"

"No," she blurted, then wished for a muzzle on her tongue. Now it was too late. But where had that denial come from?

"Thank God," he whispered, nuzzling her neck.

What had she done? she asked herself, clutching his back while staring at the tall cottonwoods and evergreens looming over them, their fullness and height almost enough to hide the blue sky. How different, but how exciting to make love on the hard ground, she thought, under the open sky, with so much stillness around them, like an outdoor cathedral.

Could she indeed be happy here? Forever? It was peaceful—no noise, no suspicions, no mean-spirited people, no muggings....

Was such a thing possible? Was a future possible with this man?

Over the next few days their life seemed to smooth out somewhat, for which Jeremiah felt relieved. With that relief came an odd peace of mind. After teaching Bridget how to mount Mackie and stay atop him, he'd taken her to the pasture with him two days in a row, showing her the herd of cattle he was so proud of and had such great financial hopes for.

But it was the rundown condition of the acreage that she had commented on.

"I don't pretend to know much about ranching, but why haven't you fixed all those broken fences?"

"Money, or rather, the lack of it." His tone was bleak.

"I'm . . . sorry. It looks like I've put my big foot in my mouth again."

"It's no big deal. Besides, you don't have a big foot."

She gave him a shadowy smile. "I thought you had a helper."

"I do, only he's a friend who does what he can when he can."

"I see."

"Ah, don't you worry. It'll all work out. When I take my herd to market, I'll have money to make repairs and do some other things I need to do."

"I hope everything works out for you."

He'd wanted to say, "don't you mean *us*," but he couldn't get the words out. They stuck like a boulder in his throat; he feared there would never be an us— not in the true sense of the word.

But he hadn't let those fears dampen his enthusiasm for having her with him, nor his lust for her in bed.

Beyond that lust, he didn't know how he felt. Love was no longer a part of his vocabulary, although he couldn't say that being married to Margaret had left a bad taste in his mouth. It hadn't. While he hadn't loved her the way he should have, he had depended on her.

In every sense of the word, Margaret had been a rancher's wife. She knew how to do what needed to be done. He'd worked from daylight until dark almost every day, and when he came in, the house was immaculate, the food was on the table, and if he wanted sex, then she would accommodate him with that, too.

But now, after Bridget had come into his life, he knew he'd just existed with Margaret, that he hadn't been alive. Bridget made him feel and see things that had once been a blur.

Had he fallen in love? No way. He was sure of that. Hell, he didn't even know if he was capable of loving. He figured he was too weak and selfish. If that wasn't the case, he would never have sent . . .

Shaking his head, Jeremiah dumped that train of thought, unable to deal with it now, but knowing that sooner or later he was going to have to. The knowledge that he hadn't was eating at his insides and making him feel not only guilty but like a heel, as well.

Anyway, his gut told him that one day Bridget would leave. Right now she was hiding from something; he didn't know what, and she wouldn't confide in him. He could understand that; hell, he hadn't confided in her either. But in his own defense, she hadn't even been there quite two weeks.

Still, the thought of losing her, the thought of waking up and not having her beside him in bed, made him physically sick.

Now, as he stepped into the shower after a hard day branding cattle, he paused, realizing he smelled something. Food? He wrinkled his nose. Was Bridget actually cooking?

He grinned, unable to imagine how it would taste, but it didn't matter. "Well, I'll be damned." She was cooking, and that was all that counted. Then cursing, he cautioned himself for giving in to that false sense of complacency again.

"You'd best get ready, old boy, 'cause it's not going to last," he muttered before reaching for the soap. "You showed your tail when you took part in that auction."

Talking to himself somehow quieted the churning inside, and for a moment he was content to feel the sting of the water on his tired body.

It was at that moment that he heard the click of the shower door. He swung around. Bridget stood there, beautiful, like a goddess. And naked. He felt instantly aroused, and knew that she noticed it, too.

She smiled, then asked, "Want some company?"

"Oh, baby, you don't know how much."

Closing the door behind her, she stepped under the water with him, wrapping her hand around his fledgling hardness.

"Oh, my, my," he whispered, expelling a shuddering breath. "What you do to me."

A long while later, she was the first to get out and dry off. Even after pounding himself hard inside her against the wall of the shower, he wasn't too tired to appreciate her perfect derriere as she bent over and dried her toes.

"Mmm, that's nice," he said, turning off the faucet.

She smiled and wrinkled her nose. "Don't you ever get enough?"

"Of you? No."

Her faced turned red. "I—"

The phone rang, stopping her mid-sentence, which was just as well, Jeremiah told himself. He figured he wouldn't have liked what she was about to say. He didn't want anything to spoil the uneasy truce between them.

"Would you get that?" he asked, reaching for his towel. "It's probably Irma inviting us to the church social."

"If it is, you want to go?"

"Sure, if you do."

She didn't respond. Instead, she raced for the phone.

He couldn't hear what was being said, nor did he care. He was too busy humming, thinking he was about the luckiest fellow in the world at that moment. Bridget was still his wife, still in his house, still in his bed. What more could a man ask for?

To hell with tomorrow; it would take care of itself.

"Jeremiah?"

He stopped drying his toes and straightened. "Hell, I guess I gotta go talk, right?"

"No."

His eyebrow rose. "Then it was for you?"

"No, actually, it was for you."

"Who was it?" He frowned. "Are they still on the line?"

"It was your aunt, and, no, she's not on the line."

His heart skipped a beat, but he ignored it, forcing his voice to remain even. "Ah, so she's back home."

"Where's she been?"

"Gone to visit her brother... my uncle."

"I was wondering why you never introduced her to me."

"So did you introduce yourself?" His tone was guarded.

"Yes, as a matter of fact, I did."

"As my wife?"

"Yes."

His heart skipped two beats this time. "And what did she say?"

"I think she was taken aback, but she handled it well." Bridget's eyes were troubled. "But the reason she called is not so good. She fell and broke her leg right after she got home."

Jeremiah cursed, then swallowed the bile that flooded the back of his throat. "Good Lord! Where is she now?"

"At home. Apparently a close neighbor, a widow, is staying with her."

"Why the hell didn't she call me last night?"

"You'll have to ask her that." Bridget paused, then cocked her head. "She said something else."

Jeremiah's heart no longer beat. "What?" he asked, but he knew.

"She said you'd have to come and get Taylor."

He blew out a harsh breath and shifted his gaze.

"Jeremiah, who's Taylor?"

He turned around, knowing the misery he was feeling showed in his eyes.

"Jeremiah?"

"Taylor's my five-year-old daughter."

Fifteen

Bridget stared at him, dumbfounded. When she tried to speak, her mouth opened, then closed.

"I know I should've told you," Jeremiah said, looking down and hitching the towel around his waist.

In that moment when their eyes lost contact, Bridget took a deep breath and tried to regain her composure. She couldn't. She felt dizzy and nauseous. Her breathing deepened as she fought to avoid running to the commode to throw up.

A child! Jeremiah had a *child*. That in itself was not so mind-boggling, but the fact that he hadn't told her—even when she'd all but asked—was. No, mind-boggling wasn't the correct word. Actually, there were so many colorful adjectives that fit the feelings warring inside her that she couldn't begin to settle on one.

"You lied to me," she said, jerking her head up and glowering at him.

He flinched as if she'd hit him. Good. She couldn't tolerate liars, and in her book, Jeremiah Davis was a liar.

"I think that word's a little strong."

She laughed with no humor. "Oh, you do, do you?" she countered, near hysterics. "God, how could you—"

Jeremiah held up his hand, his features pale and grim, and cut her off. "Look, if we're going to go the inquisition route, then I'd like to dress."

"Then dress, damn you!"

With that she turned, dashed into the bedroom and slammed the door behind her. But she didn't move; she leaned against it and fought tears, that helpless, panicked sickness moving from her stomach into her chest. She wouldn't have a panic attack. *She wouldn't.*

She clenched her fists and took several deep, unhurried breaths. Finally the dizziness abated somewhat, and she no longer trembled. She wouldn't give him the satisfaction of knowing that he had knocked the props out from under her world.

Here she'd been thinking that maybe they had a future together, that she could remain in this godforsaken no-man's-land and be happy. She should have known better. She should have known he wasn't the man he appeared to be.

Damn, but she felt like a fool. A child. She didn't know the first thing about taking care of a child. The thought of being responsible for a five-year-old scared the hell out of her. It wasn't the child's age that had her spooked, either—being responsible for *any* child, no matter the age, evoked the same emotion.

Still, it wasn't so much the child as the feeling of betrayal that had crushed her. She thought she'd found a diamond in the rough in Jeremiah Davis. What she'd found was a liar. What else was he hiding?

Bridget pushed herself away from the door just as she heard the knob turn. Moving to the middle of the room, she faced him when he walked in, dressed only in his underwear.

"I thought you were going to get dressed," she snapped.

He cursed. "Not in the bathroom. My clothes just happen to be in here. Besides, I am dressed."

"Right."

He cursed at her heated sarcasm. She turned away, unwilling to let his bare chest and hard, muscled thighs distract her from her mission, which was to find out *why* he'd lied to her.

She sensed he would like to throttle her, only that wasn't his style. Besides, he knew he was the one in the wrong; it was obvious in the deepening lines around his mouth and eyes, not to mention the hangdog expression on his face.

She watched as he crossed to the closet, knowing that she was probably being unreasonable, but she didn't care. She was in such a state of fury and shock that she refused to cut him any slack at all.

"Well, I guess this is the moment we've been waiting for," he said minutes later, after putting on jeans and a shirt. "The part where you fade into the sunset."

Bridget's fury mounted. "How dare you joke about this?"

"Trust me, I'm not," he said on a sigh, leaning against the wall. "My daughter's anything but a joke."

"So when were you going to tell me?" Bridget began to shake again. She folded her arms across her chest so that he wouldn't notice.

He looked away, then at her. "What would you have done if I had?"

"Oh, no, you don't." Bridget's eyes flashed. "I want an answer to *my* question."

"All right. Lord knows, you deserve one." Jeremiah rubbed his chin. "I don't know."

"Is that your answer?" Her voice remained high-pitched, but she didn't care.

"Look, of course, I was going to tell you, only I—" He broke off, tightening his lips.

"Only what?" she asked. "How could you possibly hide something like a child, for God's sake?"

"I wasn't sure you'd be here long enough, that's why!"

For a moment, she didn't know what to say; she was too astounded. Then she saw the look on his face and heard the anger in his voice. Damn him! she thought. He was in the wrong, not her.

"So you thought that, in the meantime, you'd just keep your child a secret?"

"Hell, Bridget," he said, his tone low and full of agony, "it wasn't like that."

"Then how was it?" she asked in a dull voice.

"When Margaret died, I went into a funk, in every sense of the word. I was lonely. I was having financial difficulties, even more than now. Just paying for the funeral nearly broke me." He paused and averted his gaze. "Then I started drinking, feeling sorry for myself."

"So your aunt took Taylor." It wasn't a question but a flat statement of fact.

"That's about the size of it. I wasn't a fit parent. Taylor needed a woman, or at least I thought so at the time."

"But it's been years, Jeremiah. How could you stay away from your daughter that long?"

He shoved one hand through his hair, then stared at her through tortured eyes. "I haven't been away from her, not in the sense you mean. I visit her at my aunt's at least twice a week, sometimes more. But right before the auction, my aunt went to see her brother and, of course, she took Taylor with her, since she's only in kindergarten."

Bridget shook her head as if to digest what he'd told her. She couldn't. She wasn't a parent, but she still couldn't understand how he could let someone else rear his child.

"I know what you're thinking, that I'm a first-class heel."

She flushed, but she didn't wince. "Yes."

"At the time I did what I thought was best for my child. I'd just lost my wife, her mother." Jeremiah straightened, and his voice hardened. "I won't pretend that I haven't made mistakes. I'm far from a perfect parent, but I did what I thought was best."

"And you make no apologies for it, is that it?"

"Hell, I told you, I went berserk. I couldn't even stand to look at Margaret's picture. It was as though she'd left me on purpose."

So that was why there were no pictures of his family around, Bridget thought before switching her mind back on track.

"I'm sorry for your loss, but that still doesn't excuse your lying to me."

His head jerked, and his eyes narrowed. "I didn't lie."

"Yes, you did. You told me those toys in that spare room belonged to a friend's child."

"Okay, so that was a mistake. I'll admit that I just couldn't tell you. But what about you? Can you tell me that you've been completely honest with me, that you don't have any deep dark secrets that you'd rather I didn't know?"

"Well, I can assure you that *I* don't have a child!"

He drew back.

"Didn't you think I had the right to know?"

He massaged his temple, looking miserable. "Of course you did, but I couldn't find the words to tell you. And when I thought I had them, they stuck in my throat."

"Why, Jeremiah?" Her voice was so low, she thought he might not have heard her.

"Because at first, I . . . I was afraid I'd lose you."

She moistened her lips. "That's because you never had me."

"Dammit, Bridget, don't—"

She turned and walked toward the door.

"Bridget!"

Later, she didn't know what made her stop and listen. At the time, it seemed the only thing to do. "What?"

"Will you go with me to get Taylor? Please."

She eased around and watched as he blinked once, twice, then shook his head, as if the tumult of his emotions had caused his vision to blur.

Masking a crippling sense of pain, she nodded.

"Is that a yes?" His voice shook.

She took a steadying breath. "That's a yes."

Lilah Davis's house was just as Bridget had pictured it after Jeremiah's description of her as they drove—small, but tastefully decorated and immaculately clean.

Now, as she sat in front of the woman who had reared Jeremiah, practically the only mother he'd ever had, Bridget didn't know what to say.

Lilah didn't seem to have that problem. "I'm sorry we had to meet under such terrible circumstances."

"Me, too."

Jeremiah and Taylor had gone into the bedroom to pack the child's bags. Lilah had asked Bridget to fix some coffee for the two of them, and she had obliged, glad of something, anything, to occupy her hands. Too bad her mind couldn't be otherwise occupied.

"It's time, you know. She should be with him."

Bridget smiled at the woman, who was in her seventies but could have passed for fifty. Her figure was trim, her hair totally without gray, and her face unlined. Bridget knew that Jeremiah favored her a great deal, but more important was the love they had for one another.

"I agree, and I told him as much." Bridget paused and sipped her coffee. "But now I'm thinking perhaps I was too hasty, too judgmental. You seem to have been perfect for her."

"She's certainly filled the last stages of my life. Since I never married, Taylor's been the grandchild I never had."

"What will you do now?"

Lilah smiled. "I've been preparing for this day, though not in quite this way."

"No, I'd think not," Bridget said, taking in the cast on Lilah's leg, which was propped on a chair, her crutches nearby.

"But I'll be fine. Having been a nurse for thirty years, I know the drill. And until I get this darn thing off my leg, I'll hire a companion." She turned and faced the bedroom. "I just hope you and Taylor will become friends."

"I'm sure we will," Bridget said, shifting her gaze, all the while thinking she was living another nightmare.

"By the way," Lilah was saying, "have I told you how glad I am that Jeremiah married you?"

"But you don't know me. How can..."

"So far, I like what I see. Besides, I've never seen Jeremiah like this before. I've never seen that 'look' on his face. You've made him happy."

Only in bed, which isn't enough, Bridget thought, guilt crushing her chest. "You didn't object to the auction in Pennington? I mean..." Again her voice faded.

"No, I thought it was a great idea." Lilah chuckled. "Although I have to say, I was knocked for a loop when I found out he'd married you."

"So was I."

Lilah's eyes widened. "Excuse me?"

"Nothing. I was just teasing." *Now who's lying?*

"So what do you think about our Taylor? Isn't she a darling?"

That she was, Bridget conceded, a precocious darling, at that. When they had parked in the driveway, the door had no sooner been flung open than the child bounced out to the car.

Jeremiah had lost no time in getting out and sweeping her into his arms. Only after he'd set her down had Bridget gotten a good look at Taylor. She was tiny, even for her age, with straight brown hair, light brown eyes and a sprinkling of freckles across her nose.

"Who are you?" she'd asked, her eyes curious.

Bridget had smiled for lack of anything better to do.

"Taylor, honey, it's not nice to be so blunt," Jeremiah had said, looking as ill at ease as Bridget felt. "Come on, let's get your things packed. While we're doing that, I'll share a secret with you."

He'd looked at Bridget then, as only he could. Her heart raced, which she saw as a betrayal by her body. She wanted to despise this man for what he'd done. But she couldn't.

"Come on, let's get inside."

That conversation had taken place thirty minutes ago, and the two of them were still in Taylor's room. And Lilah was staring at her with a strange expression on her face.

"You didn't hear what I just said, did you?"

Color stole into Bridget's face. "Sorry, I was thinking about something else."

Lilah laughed. "That's all right. It wasn't important. I just—"

Her words were cut off as Jeremiah and Taylor walked into the living room. He smiled at Lilah. "We've got everything packed."

"Then you should be on your way." Lilah's voice shook.

Bridget stood and looked at Jeremiah. "I'll wait outside."

Lilah smiled her thanks.

"You know what?"

"No, what?"

"My mommy's an angel."

Bridget's heartstrings jerked, and for a moment she felt the threat of tears. They were in the car, heading to the ranch. She knew without being told that Jeremiah had informed his daughter that he had married again, though Taylor hadn't said one word about it. In fact, this was the first time she'd spoken directly to Bridget.

She willed back the tears, hating herself for her inability to keep her emotions under better control.

"Sweetheart," Jeremiah said, "I've told you not to—"

Bridget shook her head. "It's okay." Then, to the child, she said, "Your mommy's a lucky lady."

"She's in heaven with Jesus."

Bridget heard Jeremiah's quiet moan.

"That makes it even better."

"Do you have any children?"

"No."

"Oh."

Bridget forced a smile. "Is that bad?"

"Nah, 'cept I get lonesome sometimes."

"I bet you have lots of friends, though."

Taylor shrugged her tiny shoulders. "Sandy's my best friend, but I won't get to see her anymore."

"Yes, you will," Jeremiah put in, his tone bordering on desperation. "Every time you see Mama Lilah, you can see Sandy."

Taylor didn't say anything.

"I'm sure you'll make new friends at your new school," Bridget said, desperately trying to ease both the awkward silence and the building tension. Why hadn't she packed her bags and walked out the door? She knew Jeremiah had expected her to do just that. So why hadn't she?

"We're home," Jeremiah announced suddenly, in a voice that left no doubt he was at his wits' end.

They were silent when they walked into the house; then Jeremiah lifted Taylor. "It's bedtime for you, young lady."

"Do I have to?" she whined.

"Yep. It's been a long day for all of us."

Once Taylor was in his arms, she looked at Jeremiah, then at Bridget, her eyes sober. "Daddy said that you're my new mommy."

Sixteen

She was going to kill him. She didn't know how yet, but she would do it regardless of the consequences. The thought of making him suffer a slow, painful death made her feel better.

How dare he tell that child that she was her new mommy? She hadn't even forgiven him for keeping the child's existence from her, for heaven's sake. Now he'd just told Taylor that she had a new mother. As if she was going to be there forever.

Bridget stopped pacing, feeling the knot in her stomach give a brutal twist. If she was going to leave, she should do it this minute. She should march into that bedroom, grab her suitcase, toss her clothes into it, then walk out.

Did she do that? No, she just stood there in the middle of the living room and fumed, like some crazed teenager who had been stood up on her first date.

Damn! She was a grown woman; she didn't need this slow-moving cowboy to make her life complete. She could return to Houston and start over. That thought brightened her spirits, but only for a second. She didn't want—

"I'm surprised you're still here."

She whirled and stared at Jeremiah, who was leaning against the doorjamb.

"I am, too, if you want to know the truth."

"You're mad, aren't you?"

"That doesn't even come close to how I feel."

"Dammit, Bridget, I had to tell her something."

Bridget almost choked. "How about the truth? But then, you wouldn't know that if it—"

Two long strides brought him so close to her that her next words clogged in her throat. But he didn't touch her, though she sensed he wanted to. His grim features were a giveaway.

"Don't say it. Don't even think it. I'm no liar and you know it. You're my *wife,* so that makes you her mother, or at least that's the way I see it."

"Stepmother."

"That's splitting hairs, and you know it."

This conversation had gotten way out of hand, and Bridget was clueless as to how to cool their tempers and bring things into perspective. Anything said at this point had the potential to explode like a lighted stick of dynamite.

"Look," Jeremiah said, as if he had again picked up on what was galloping through her mind, "I know I came on kind of strong, but when she asked about you and what you were doing here, I just blurted it out." His voice sounded scratchy, as if he needed to cough. "I'm sorry. I know I had no right."

He seemed so unsure of himself in that moment, so vulnerable, that she almost capitulated and let him get away with what he'd done. She fought the urge to put her arms around his shoulders and press his head against her breast.

Only she couldn't. She couldn't let him or his child think that she could ever be a mommy to Taylor, or to any other child. Granted, she had nothing against children, and had at one time even dreamed of having one of her one. Now she knew that wasn't possible.

She had two major strikes against her, which made her afraid to have a child. She'd had no role model, as her own mother hadn't known how to be a parent. And someone who was subject to anxiety attacks couldn't and shouldn't be a mother.

There! She'd finally faced that brutal truth! That was one of the reasons she'd put off Hamilton...among others. She knew he would want a houseful of children, and she knew she wouldn't be a good mother.

"So, are you leaving?"

Bridget ground her teeth together. "Give me a good reason I shouldn't."

"We're married."

"That can easily be changed."

"Right, it can," he muttered, his tone harsh.

Silence.

"So, you're going back to the easy life and the cement?"

She didn't answer. She couldn't. One minute she wanted to stay, the next she wanted to go. But then, those erratic emotions had been there inside her from the first moment she'd seen this man.

He cupped his hand around her elbow. "I need you, Bridget." His voice was soft and gentle, with an almost timid quality.

She looked at his hand, then up. "Is that your way of asking me to stay?"

His eyes were compelling. "Yes."

That simple word, so loaded with meaning, hung between them. And when he looked at her like that, she couldn't deny him anything.

"All right, I'll stay," she said through dry lips. "But you can't expect me—"

He held up his hands, stopping her. "I know. I can't expect you to be Taylor's mother."

Spoken out loud, those words sounded so cold-hearted, so inhuman. But she couldn't let him have false hope that she could replace his wife in every sense of the word. At best their relationship was tenuous and could end at any time. She couldn't set herself up for further pain. Her old wounds were just now healing.

"I'm . . . sorry," she whispered at last.

"Don't be. I understand." His eyes connected with hers. "So where do we go from here?"

"We take one day at a time."

Another week passed, bringing her stay to three in total. During that time, the trio settled into a pattern of seminormality, which in itself was a surprise. There had actually been hours in which she and Jeremiah had gotten along. Still, she hadn't kidded herself. Their situation remained volatile and had the potential to blow up every time they were in the same room.

But what was more of a surprise than the surface calm between her and Jeremiah was her attitude toward the child. Taylor had managed to worm her way into her heart, and she was smitten with her, even though she really didn't know any more about rearing children than she did about gardening or cooking.

That didn't seem to matter, not with Taylor, anyway, who seemed to accept her with the love and eagerness of a child who was desperate to be like other children, to have a mother, though she hadn't actually called her Mommy.

Bridget felt Jeremiah had put the damper on that, which was the right thing to do. Taylor had already suffered enough bruises in her short life. Bridget didn't want to be responsible for more. Besides, when she left, she didn't want to carry guilt home in addition to her other luggage.

Remaining here was about dropping baggage, not adding to it.

"My, but you're quiet," Jeremiah said one night in bed.

Bridget smiled, then stretched. When she did, a breast was exposed, sliding out from under the cover.

Jeremiah leaned over and tongued it.

"Mmm, that's good," she said.

He lifted his head, his eyes hot. "You're telling me."

"How could either one of us want any more?"

"I never get tired of burying myself inside you."

"I never get tired of feeling you inside me, either," she whispered.

They had gone to bed early, just after dark, both tired from the day's activities. Jeremiah, with some money he'd made from the sale of a few head of cattle, had spent the day mending fences. As a favor, Bridget had gone into town and helped Irma open freight in the store, then helped her put the items on the shelves.

But they hadn't been too tired to make love.

Now, Bridget was in a quandary. She had told him they should take it one day at a time. But she was feeling that ticking clock. What was she going to do? Was she going to remain here, as his wife? Without love, was that possible?

The phone rang, jarring her to reality.

"Damn," Jeremiah muttered, voicing her thoughts.

So as not to awaken Taylor, Bridget reached for the receiver on the second ring. "Hello," she said, hearing the breathlessness in her voice as Jeremiah's tongue moved down her stomach.

"Bridget, is that you?"

"Hello, Daddy."

Jeremiah's tongue seemed to freeze, and he looked up, his eyes unreadable.

"When are you coming home? This charade has gone far enough. Your mother's having a terrible time dealing with you living there, with that . . . man."

She knew Jeremiah could hear every word Allen Martin spouted, because his face turned granite hard, and his lips stretched into a thin, white line.

"Daddy, now's not a good time for us to talk. I'll call you back."

"No. We have to settle this now. There's no excuse for your behavior."

"I don't have to offer any excuses, Daddy." Bridget steeled herself against his verbal attack. "It's *my* life."

"That's why I hate to see you mess it up." Allen paused. "There's someone here who wants to speak to you. I've given up trying to talk some sense into you."

Jeremiah mouthed "good," which brought a smile to Bridget's lips, but it disappeared when she heard the next voice.

"Hello, Hamilton."

Jeremiah cursed.

"Bridget, what the hell's going on?" he demanded. "I can't believe you're still holed up in that hick town with that—"

"It's not a good time for us to talk, either," she said, cutting him off. "I promise I'll call you back."

While he was still sputtering, Bridget replaced the receiver, then turned to Jeremiah, who was watching her.

The hot night beat all around them.

"Why did you really come here?"

His words stabbed at her heart. "I needed a place to heal."

"Why? Were you sick?"

"Are you familiar with anxiety attacks?"

"Yeah. One of the men who participated in the auction has them."

"Well, I do, too, terrible ones. So terrible, in fact, that I'm on medication, which is why I got so tipsy the night I came here."

"I'm sorry," he said. "No one deserves that curse."

"It's a curse, all right, only I couldn't wallow in self-pity. I had to find a way to deal with it."

"So you came here, where the pace is less hectic and the living is easy? Is that what you're saying?"

She looked away from his penetrating gaze. "That's right."

Jeremiah tugged at her chin, drawing her around to face him. "Are you sure it's that simple, that something else didn't drive you here? I have this gut feeling that—"

"Forget your gut feeling. There's nothing else," she said, without so much as blinking. She almost told him about the lawsuit, but something stopped her. It was a can of worms she would rather not reopen, especially when she didn't have to.

"So when *are* you going to tell your parents and that jerk, Hamilton what's-his-name, that we're married?" There was anguish in his face.

"Soon."

"Promise?"

She couldn't promise. So she did the next best thing. She kissed him on the nipple, then whispered, "Make love to me again."

He groaned and did as she asked.

"Do you and my daddy have sex?"

Bridget's mouth flopped open and closed, like a guppy's, while her head reeled. When she found her voice, she asked, "Where on earth did—" She couldn't even finish the sentence. It was as though the wind had been knocked out of her.

Anyway, she didn't want to know the answer. Dear Lord, the child was only five years old and already asking about sex. What was happening to this world? Only it wasn't this world she had to worry about, just this precocious child with the serious face.

They had just come in from the garden, where Taylor had planted a row of tomatoes. Bridget had supervised, which was a joke, of course. Taylor had done all the work.

Jeremiah had come in from the pasture and checked on them from time to time; he would shake his head, grin, then meander back to his work.

Bridget had questioned Jeremiah about enrolling Taylor in kindergarten. Jeremiah had laughed and said the closest thing to that was miles away. Bridget told him that she didn't care; she would get Taylor to class, which was only in the mornings.

Now, as they sat side by side on the couch, Bridget grappled for a way to defuse the awkward situation.

"Mark told me *his* parents 'do it,'" Taylor said, ending the lengthy silence.

"Taylor!" Appalled, Bridget fought for the best way to handle this. "What is sex? Do you even know?"

Taylor was silent for a moment. "Sort of, I guess. Does it have to do with making meat loaf? Mark said—"

"Okay, that's enough of that subject, young lady," Bridget said, trying to contain the laughter that threatened to erupt. "Mark is wrong. He shouldn't be telling you what goes on between his parents."

"Why?" Her tone was guileless.

Oh, Lord, give me strength. "Because it's personal and private." Bridget knew she was botching this explanation, but she couldn't help it. She wanted to answer Taylor with as much honesty as she could, yet there was a line that she couldn't cross.

"It's also something that grown-ups share. As to your original question, yes, your daddy and I have sex, but that's because we're married and lo—" She couldn't say the word that popped into her mind, because she didn't know if it pertained to her and Jeremiah or not.

"So enough about sex. You've got a lot of years in front of you before you have to worry about that. Learning how to read and write is what you should be concerned about."

Taylor snuggled closer against her, and in spite of herself, Bridget felt her heart race. This little minx knew just the right buttons to push.

"Ah, all that stuff's a piece of cake," the child was saying. "I already know how to do all that."

Bridget reached for another book off the couch beside her. "Suppose you prove it to me, then." She tousled the child's hair.

"What's going on in here?"

At the sound of Jeremiah's voice, Bridget's head bounced up. Their eyes met over Taylor's head, and for a moment, Bridget almost stopped breathing. She could have sworn the look in his eyes spoke of love. No! She was wrong. He didn't love her; he just wanted her. She had to remember there was a difference.

"Hi, Daddy," Taylor said, shattering the tension. "I'm going to read. Want to listen?"

Jeremiah's eyes remained on Bridget. "Can't right now, sweetie. I've got to get back to the pasture. Maybe later."

"Okay," Taylor said, scooting even closer to Bridget.

Jeremiah looked at her for a moment longer, his eyes smoldering, then turned and strode off.

Afterward, it took three stories before Bridget's stampeding heart settled.

"Why, Brewer, what the hell brings you across the line?"

Reagan Brewer, the justice of the peace who had married them, smiled, though Jeremiah thought it looked mighty weak and more than a little sick.

"I need to talk to you," Brewer said, his voice sounding like rough sandpaper.

"Well, I guess I can take a break. The sun's hotter than hell. Come on, let's go stand under that cottonwood."

"Suits me," Brewer said.

"So what's up?" Jeremiah placed an arm around his old friend's shoulders as they sauntered toward the shade. "If you're here about buying some of my herd—"

"Er... this ain't about cattle."

Seconds later, Jeremiah stopped in his tracks, then hollered, "What the hell are you saying?"

Seventeen

"**D**amn, damn, damn!"

Cursing into the wind did little to unkink the knots in Jeremiah's gut. A dead bull—the sire bull, no less, that he'd purchased months ago from out of state. Following Reagan Brewer's visit yesterday, dead livestock was the last thing he needed.

Right now he couldn't worry about Brewer's bombshell. Besides, he hadn't gotten up enough courage to even think beyond that conversation, much less deal with it. He didn't have that luxury with this dead animal. His herd was his livelihood, scant as that might be, but he still couldn't afford to ignore the possibility that something besides natural causes had killed the animal.

Tuberculosis. That was the deadly disease that popped into his mind and made him turn green. If that proved to be the case, then his entire herd would have to be slaughtered. He should have recognized the symptoms early on—loss of appetite, lethargy. But no, he'd been blind to everything except Bridget. She had consumed his time, his thoughts, his *life*.

Jeremiah heard the sound of a truck behind him. Whirling, he looked on as the old veterinarian, Doc Minshew, brought his pickup to a stop.

"Hell, boy, you look like you've been eatin' bitter weeds through a picket fence," he commented, getting out, then shifting a wad of chewing tobacco to the other side of his mouth.

The old man grinned, which turned Jeremiah greener. Not only had the tobacco juice stained his teeth the color of rich cocoa, but strings of the tobacco were stuck between various teeth, reminding Jeremiah of rotten, wilted spinach.

Jeremiah almost gagged, but he managed to contain himself. What the hell was the matter with him? He knew what ailed him, all right, only he couldn't deal with it at the moment.

"Hello, Minshew," Jeremiah said, after the man hobbled toward the animal. "Mmm, looks like Ol' Arthur's got you this morning."

"Ever' morning, boy. When you git my age, arthritis gits in ever' joint, ever' nook and cranny of your body." Minshew shoved his greasy hat back, then bent over to get a closer look at the dead bull. "When did you find him?"

"Right before I sent for you."

Minshew was silent as he examined the animal from top to bottom. Then he lumbered upright again. "I have a notion as to what killed 'im, but I'll have to run some tests."

"Could it be TB?" Jeremiah's tone was flat. "Now that I think back, he had some of the symptoms."

"Yep, sure could."

"Dammit, I—" Jeremiah couldn't go on, because he knew what it meant. Still, he wasn't able to get the words past his stiff lips. Suddenly he wanted to vent his frustration and anger on any moving target, even the cantankerous old vet. Instead, he stood there, staring at the bull and seeing his whole future go down the toilet.

"Dammit!"

He hadn't realized he'd spoken again until Minshew said, "If it was me, I'd say worse, 'cause I know what this herd means to you. I know it's your livelihood."

"What livelihood?" Jeremiah's tone was bitter.

"Well, have faith, boy. Maybe it won't be so bad after all."

"Minshew, any light at the end of my tunnel's just another damned train."

Something was eating at Jeremiah besides the dead animal, but Bridget didn't know what. He wouldn't confide in her, though she'd asked him several times what was bothering him. She felt secure in probing, now that she had been in Pennington nearly a month.

It didn't seem possible, but the calendar didn't lie. For the last two weeks, they had been living as husband and wife... *family* in the truest sense of the word. Since she had made the decision not to accept that job in Houston, she had changed even more. She no longer fought the fact that she was actually enjoying life. Taylor was partly responsible; they had become even closer, though at times she'd been in a quandary as to how to cope with the child's precociousness, or the temper tantrums when she didn't get her way.

Still, the marriage was working, despite the fact that neither of them had spoken the word love, though it hovered around the edges of Bridget's mind, taunting her, working on her psyche. She suspected the same was true with Jeremiah, though she hadn't had the nerve to broach that subject for fear of snapping the fragile thread that held them together.

Too, there was still that unanswered question that nagged at her. There was so much that went into being a rancher's wife; could she learn it all? More important, was she willing to? On the heels of that question came others. Was she willing to give up everything she'd worked so long and hard for to remain here as a wife and mother? Was her inability to answer those questions the reason she hadn't told her parents the truth? Yes, she admitted to herself.

Yet when Jeremiah held her and kissed her, she felt she would be content to remain here in his arms forever.

Now, as she watched her husband sit down at the table after a shower and a long day outdoors, her main concern was removing that worried, hangdog expression on his face.

"I made a casserole for dinner."

He actually smiled. "What did you leave out this time?"

That question resulted from two days ago when she'd cooked dinner, only to have Taylor say, "Yuck, this tastes awful." Come to find out, Bridget had left out the main ingredient, something she knew would take her a long time to live down.

She placed her hands on her hips, then thrust the right one toward him. "I'm going to have to do something about that smart mouth of yours."

His eyes glittered, while his voice turned into a hoarse croak. "Come here."

On unsteady legs, Bridget walked to him. Without taking his eyes off her, he pulled her onto his lap. She felt his arousal and matched it with a heat of her own.

"How 'bout skipping dinner and going immediately to dessert?" he whispered, nuzzling her neck and surrounding a breast with one hand.

"I . . . we don't have dessert."

"That's where you're wrong. *You're* the dessert—mine, anyway."

Only because Taylor was spending the night with a friend were they able to behave like this, except in the bedroom, where never a night passed that he didn't make love to her, even when he was in his present dark mood.

"I've always wanted to make love to you in a chair."

"That's about the only place we haven't done it." Bridget's husky tone matched his.

"Well, I guess now's the time to correct that oversight."

His hand had found its way under her T-shirt. "I love it when you don't wear a bra."

She chuckled. "I've learned it's a waste of time. You just take it off every chance you get."

"Which isn't nearly often enough."

She pulled back. "Why, Jeremiah Davis, that's a fib, and you know it."

He had her shirt up now and was kneading both breasts. "Have I told you that these are incredible?"

"Not since this morning."

He drew her head down then and kissed her. For a reason she couldn't explain, Bridget sensed a desperation in the hot urgency of his mouth. When the kiss ended, they were so breathless that for a moment they couldn't speak.

Then Bridget whispered, "I know you're upset about the herd, but don't be. I have some . . . money."

The hand on her breast stilled. "Sorry, no can do."

"But—"

"Forget it, honey, that's a dead subject. If the herd's sick and has to be destroyed, then I'll just start over."

This time *she* kissed *him*. Hard. "You're the most stubborn man I've ever known."

He smiled, though it didn't reach his eyes. "So what are you going to do about it?"

"Pound some of that stubbornness out of you, I guess."

"Ah, a lady after my own heart."

"You're—"

The phone rang.

"Hellfire!"

Bridget giggled. "We have to answer it. It might be your aunt, or Taylor."

He lifted her off his lap, then stood, though his gaze remained on her, hot and glazed.

Only after he lifted the receiver did that expression change. Bridget watched as he seemed to hold his breath.

"Well, I'll be damned," he finally said, grinning from ear to ear.

Bridget didn't have to ask who the caller was or what he wanted. The cattle were okay, her instinct told her. Thank God, she thought, even as he replaced the receiver, grabbed her and swung her around.

"Whoopee! The bull died from natural causes. No TB."

"Oh, Jeremiah, that's wonderful!"

"We have to celebrate, of course, only there's something I should tell you."

Again she saw *that* look on his face, and an uneasy feeling washed through her. Yet as much as she wanted him to tell her what was bothering him, she felt it could wait a bit longer. After all, he'd aroused her body to a feverish pitch, and they *did* have to celebrate.

"Now? Can't it wait?" She ran her tongue across his lower lip and heard him suck in his breath. "As I recall, we have a date."

His face cleared, and he laughed, backing her toward that chair.

"Who?" Bridget asked into the receiver.

"Lynette Scarbrough. Surely you remember me?"

"I'm sorry." Bridget inhaled. "Of course I remember you. You...you just caught me off guard, that's all."

"That's good, because I took the liberty of tracking down your friend Tiffany, and she gave me this number."

Bridget had to sit on the side of the bed; then she turned and stared at the bathroom, where she could hear the water as well as see Jeremiah's silhouette in the shower. She was thankful he was occupied and that it was late enough that Taylor was already in bed.

"Uh, so what can I do for you?"

Minutes later, Bridget stood in the middle of the room, her mind in an uproar. Jeremiah chose that moment to come waltzing out of the bathroom, naked as usual, only to pull up short.

"What's wrong?"

"I just got off the phone."

"So, who was it? You look like someone just cut your throat."

"Thanks."

"Well, you do." There was a stubborn, unapologetic note in his voice.

"There's something that I should have told you, only I didn't."

He shrugged. "I'm not surprised. I knew you were holding out on me."

"Now's not the time for sarcasm, Jeremiah."

"You're right." His eyes were hooded. "So, let's hear it."

She told him about the sexual harassment suit, watching his face for his reaction. She got nothing until she was finished.

"Give me five minutes with that bastard, and he wouldn't have to worry about hurting another woman. I'd castrate him like a bull, then listen while he sang soprano in his church choir."

"That's what he deserves, so that's why I have no choice but to go back to Houston."

His entire body jerked. "What?"

That word fell between them like a boulder through a glass roof.

"That creep has to be stopped, Jeremiah." Her tone was soft, yet pleading. "Especially since he's up to his old tricks. And as long as Lynette's willing to testify, I have to take advantage of that."

"Why?"

Bridget quelled her frustration. "Why? I just told you why. Besides the fact that he's a pervert, he smeared my good name and cost me my career. He has to pay for that."

"Ah, so revenge is now more important than me."

"I didn't say that." Her voice shook.

"Yes, you did. Maybe not in those exact words, but you said it—loud and clear."

"You're wrong."

"Okay, so tell me where this leaves me? Us?"

Bridget's frustration level rose. It was obvious that he had erected a mental block against everything she had said. "Look, nothing has changed. As soon as the trial's over, I'll come back to you and Taylor."

His jaw set. "Sure you will."

"Damn you! Don't you dare make this harder than it already is."

"Then why go at all?" he asked her. "Why not let this other woman testify and nail the SOB?"

"Because the law doesn't work that way. *I* have to refile the suit, and besides that, I want to be there when he gets his comeuppance." She lifted her chin with defiance. "You weren't the one whose name he dragged through the mud."

"Compared to what we have together, that shouldn't matter."

Just what do we have? she wanted to cry out. He'd never said he loved her, nor did he now. But then, she'd never told him that she loved him, either. She did, though; she knew that now, standing there, looking at him. Oh, God, she felt sick.

"One has nothing to do with the other," she whispered at last.

Panic flared in his eyes; she saw it, fleeting though it was. "Oh, it has everything to do with us. If you leave, you won't come back. Ever."

"That's ridiculous. Of course, I'll come back."

When he didn't respond and she saw the mistrust mirrored in his eyes, pain sliced through her. She wet her lips. "What are you really saying?"

"If you leave, you might as well not bother to come back."

"Don't," she said in a raw, unnatural tone. "Don't do this."

"Anyway, you're free to do as you please. Even if I wanted to stop you, I couldn't. Legally."

Bridget felt an onslaught of tears. She could barely speak. "What...what are you saying? You're not making sense."

"Reagan Brewer, the JP who married us, came to see me the other day."

"And?"

"It seems that the bastard was drunk at the time and shouldn't have married us." Jeremiah's face was wooden, and his voice sounded dead. "You see, he lost the election last fall so he didn't have the authority to do what he did."

Bridget's hand flew to her chest. She felt as though she was having a heart attack. "You...you mean..."

"Yeah, that's exactly what I mean. We aren't legally married."

Eighteen

Sweat glistened on the hairs on his chest and trickled down his face. Jeremiah paused, swiped his hand across his forehead, then glared at the sky. Damn, it was hot, he thought, but that didn't stop him from piercing another piece of wood with the ax.

The pecan tree had been struck by lightning two days ago. Rather than burn it now, out in the orchard, he'd decided to chop it into small logs for the fireplace, although he had wood stacked to the ceiling in the barn. That didn't matter; he planned to share with Irma and any other friends who needed wood. What did matter was the physical exercise and how it affected him. Thank God, it provided him with at least a minimum of relief.

His game plan was to be so tired at night that he would fall into bed in an exhaustion-induced stupor, though only after he spent time with Taylor, supervising her bath, then reading to her.

Still, he hadn't been able to sleep worth a damn. Every time he closed his eyes, he saw Bridget's face. Blinded now by the sun—or was it tears?—he slammed the ax into another piece of wood.

He shouldn't have been surprised when he'd awakened the morning following his bombshell, two weeks ago today, and found her gone. After their row, she'd slept in the other bedroom, which he'd expected. Still, when he had knocked on the door after coming in from feeding the livestock and she hadn't answered, a feeling of doom had spread through him.

He'd walked into the room and been assaulted by her scent. Muttering a groan, he'd dropped onto the bed where she'd slept and given in to the despair and fear that washed through him. That was when he had noticed the note. "I called Irma to come and get me. Please give Taylor my love."

Another groan had rocked him, and he'd crumpled the paper into a tiny wad. Taylor! God, how could he tell her that Bridget was gone? Doing so had proven to be as difficult as he'd suspected. Taylor had been a baby when her mother died, but at five years old, she knew what was going on.

"Bridget's gone away, honey," he'd said, knowing he wasn't handling the delicate situation in the right way. But it was the only way he knew—nothing he could say or do would lessen the pain for either of them.

"Did she die, Daddy?"

Taylor was sitting in his lap and staring at him with big brown eyes filled with tears. Dragging air through his burning lungs, he managed to say, "No, sweetheart, she's not dead."

"Then why did she go away? I thought she liked us."

"Oh, she did. She liked *you* a lot."

Tears soaked the child's cheeks, and she wailed, "Then why did she go away?"

"You have to understand that she wasn't used to this kind of life, that she wasn't cut out to be a rancher's wife."

"Why not?" Taylor's eyes brightened. "She was learning to cook real good, and she could hoe, too." She paused with a frown. "Only not very good."

Jeremiah wanted to smile, but he couldn't. He wasn't sure he would ever smile again, at least, not on the inside. He still felt dead in there. "There's more to living here than cooking and hoeing, sweetheart."

"I know, but—"

"Hey, it's going to be all right. You and me are going to be a team."

"I won't have to go back to Auntie's?"

"No, except just to visit. I know I haven't been a good daddy, especially after Mommy died, but for a while there I was lost, helpless. Do you understand what I'm saying? I know I'm talking to you like a grown-up, but—"

Taylor spread her tiny palm across his cheek, stopping his flow of words. "It's okay, Daddy. I *am* grown up. Bridget said so."

"Bridget said a lot of good things, but she's gone now, and we have to start over."

The child was silent while he held his breath, hoping that *he* would be enough for her.

"I'm glad, but I still want Bridget to come home." Taylor's tone was obstinate. "You told me she was my new mommy."

Jeremiah wanted to die. "She was, for a while, only it didn't work out. She . . . she had her life back in Texas."

Suddenly and unexpectedly, Taylor launched herself off his lap, then turned and glared at him through her tears. "I don't care! I want her back!"

"Taylor, please don't." He felt his insides quiver.

She placed her hands over her ears. "No!" Following that cry, she ran toward her bedroom.

"Dammit!" Jeremiah cried as the log he'd just split landed on top of his boot. His big toe caught the brunt of it. Served him right for letting his mind wander into forbidden territory.

Tossing the ax down, he limped to the nearest tree and leaned against it, cursing all the while. He removed a bandanna from his pocket and mopped his face.

At first he hadn't been too worried about Taylor. He had assumed she would rebound, as most children did. He'd been wrong. While she hadn't cried any more, there was a hollow look about her that tore at his heart.

To compound matters, he had a hell of a time comforting her, because he was in worse shape. If only he had the ability to trust. He'd had so much he loved and wanted yanked from him; it was hard for him to take circumstances and people at face value.

But his agony went deeper than mistrust. His heart felt as if Bridget had stepped on it and crushed it, which she had. He'd missed Margaret when she'd died, but it had been more for selfish reasons. She'd waited on him, done everything for him. God forgive him, he'd depended on her more than he'd loved her.

Not so with Bridget. She had a mind of her own; she was completely headstrong. And in bed she was explosive; she made *him* explode. So what did all this misery add up to? Did he love her?

Hell, yes! He had for a long time, only he'd been too pigheaded to admit it. Maybe if he had, she would still be here. No, that wasn't true. He was convinced that she could never completely adapt to his way of life, that she would soon have craved a big-city life. She had, even sooner than he'd thought.

So his only recourse—and Taylor's, too—was to go on with their lives as if she'd never been there.

And you're blowing smoke up your butt, Davis!

He didn't believe for one second that he could exist without her. Yet he had to give it a shot, for Taylor's sake if nothing else. He'd already done the unforgivable with his child—he'd let her go for two years. He couldn't afford to fail as a father again.

In order to keep from banging himself up anymore, Jeremiah stacked the wood he'd cut, then climbed on his horse and rode toward the house. A short time later, he went inside, planning to shower, then cook dinner with Taylor's help.

"Hi, Daddy," she said, her tone pensive.

"Hello, sweetheart."

She looked at him, and he noticed that her lower lip was trembling.

"What's wrong? Are you sick?"

"No."

"Then what?"

"Do...do you think Bridget would come back if you begged her to?"

Jeremiah sagged against the door. "Oh, I don't think—"

"It can't hurt to ask, can it? Can it, Daddy?"

He didn't know what to say, so he didn't say anything. He just stared at her, his mind on fire.

* * *

"What do you think? Do you like it?"

Bridget swung around and stared at her father, who stood by the window, his eyes scrutinizing her.

"It's beautiful, but—"

"Hey, no buts, just say thank-you and be done with it."

Bridget sighed, then sat in the chair behind the desk in the office that her father had found for her and furnished down to the plants in every corner and the paperweight on the desk.

"I can't, not just like that."

Allen stiffened. "Pray tell, why not? Your own practice is what you've always wanted, isn't it?"

"Yes," Bridget said, with a hesitation that wasn't lost on him.

"Well, you sure have a strange way of showing your appreciation."

"Look, Daddy, I guess what I'm trying to say is that all this is a bit overwhelming." Her eyes studied the room. "I just wasn't expecting anything like this."

A smile eased into Allen's eyes and tone. "You weren't supposed to, honey. Your mother and I wanted to surprise you."

"You certainly did that."

"Good. Now it's up to you to make the most of your new start."

"I'm not sure I can accept this, Daddy."

He was definitely taken aback; his mouth fell open, and he gulped. "What?"

"I need time."

"Time? That's crazy. You've had two weeks, for God's sake."

She couldn't argue with him, nor did she want to. What she did want was to be alone. She voiced her thoughts. "Could I have some time by myself?"

"Well, if you think it's necessary." His tone was not only haughty but miffed. "Your mother and I thought we'd take you to lunch."

"Not today, okay?"

Allen looked as though he would argue, then changed his mind. "Whatever. We'll expect to hear from you later." He got as far as the door, then turned. "I'm so glad you came to your senses and left that godforsaken place in Utah."

"Goodbye, Daddy."

He shrugged, then walked out.

Leaning back in the plush chair, Bridget let the tears that crowded her vision have free rein. Then she reached into her purse and withdrew a pill. She stared at it for a long moment, then tossed it into her mouth and swallowed it.

After she'd settled into a routine at the ranch, she'd taken no pills, which had been a blessing. But the instant she'd climbed into Irma's truck, shaking all over, she'd reached for one.

She let go a pent-up breath and once again perused the room. No finer office could be found anywhere in Houston. She was sure of that. So why didn't she feel any excitement in knowing that it was hers, that her dream of opening her own practice had become a re-ality—hers for the taking?

When she had first returned to Houston, she'd had every intention of returning to Utah, confident that Jeremiah would come to his senses and call her. When he didn't, she realized she could never return. She couldn't live with a man who couldn't trust, who lived in the past and who had never once told her he loved her.

Reaching that conclusion had broken her heart. Despite that, she had channeled that heartbreak into settling the sexual harassment lawsuit through mediation, which forced her ex-boss to make a public apology. Surprisingly, that success had been followed by several offers from prestigious law firms. She refused them all, holding on to her dream of opening her own practice.

Instead of thinking about who her first client would be and how she would handle his or her case, she was thinking about Jeremiah, wondering what *he* was doing. He was probably riding the range about this time, while Taylor was digging up worms and placing them in a jar.

Physically ill, Bridget grabbed her stomach and leaned over. She wouldn't be sick again. She couldn't, not after last night, when she'd lost everything in her stomach following a makeshift hot dog dinner at Tiffany's apartment, complete with onions, cheese and chili.

"Lord, Bridget," Tiffany had said as she held a cold washcloth to her forehead, "maybe I'd better take you to the emergency room."

"No! I'll be fine in a minute."

"Sure you will."

And she had, but only after she'd thrown up again, much to Tiffany's concern. Finally, though, when she was stretched out on the couch and had drunk some soda that had stayed down, Tiffany calmed down.

"I wish what made you sick was something as simple as a virus or my chili, but I know better."

"How do you know?"

Tiffany made a noise. "A broken heart caused you to hurl your hot dog, friend, not a virus. And there's no medicine that'll help you, either."

"Tiffany!"

"Well, it's the truth. Let's call a spade a spade here. We both know you love that cowboy. What I don't understand is why the hell you ever left him."

"He kicked me out, that's why."

"I doubt that. But if he did, I bet he didn't mean it. The man was probably scared spitless when you told him you were leaving that hole and coming back here."

"That's what he said."

"Well, I can understand that. He had already lost one person he loved. I'm sure he thought he was going to lose you to your old life."

"So what are you saying, Tiff?"

"I'm not saying anything, except, married or not, if a man looked at me like he looked at you, as though he could eat you up, I sure as hell wouldn't be *here*."

"Oh, Tiff," Bridget cried, "I don't know what to do."

Tiffany removed the washcloth and helped Bridget upright. "Yes, you do."

Bridget blinked, then swallowed. "You're right, I do. I just don't know if I can."

"You'll find a way."

Replaying that conversation in her mind forced Bridget out of the chair and over to the window. She peered outside into the stagnant Houston air and asked herself what she was doing. Her life was no longer here. Her life was in Utah. After taking the state bar exam, she could practice law there as easily as here.

Shaking all over, she grabbed the keys off the desk and dashed for the door.

"Final call for Western Airlines flight 404. All passengers holding tickets for Western flight 404, please board the aircraft."

Thank goodness, Bridget thought, after sitting through an hour delay. Later, she didn't know what made her look up the concourse, but she did.

No, she told herself, shaking her head. It couldn't be. She was seeing things. That couldn't be Jeremiah striding toward her. Why, whoever he was, he hadn't even seen her. When the man walked within shouting distance of her, she saw that it *was* Jeremiah, in the flesh, moving fast and staring straight ahead.

She feared she might faint, yet she couldn't sit down. She had to do something. She had to get his attention.

"Jeremiah!"

He stopped, turned, then watched as she walked toward him.

"Oh, God, Bridget, tell me I'm not seeing things."

"I'm real," she whispered, reaching out and touching him on the chest.

He trapped her hand against his heart, a heart that was thudding. He opened his mouth, but nothing came out.

"But how...why are you here?" she stammered. "I don't understand."

He cleared his throat. "Taylor. She's responsible. She told me I should ask you to come back, that she loved you."

"What about you? Do you love me?"

"More than life itself."

"And I love you."

He kissed her then, in the middle of the concourse. Breathless, they finally broke apart, and she looked at him with her heart reflected in her eyes. "So, what happens now?"

"That depends. Do you want to do it right this time?" He gently pushed her away, then peered into her eyes.

"Are you saying what I think you're saying?" Her voice shook.

"Yep. I thought maybe we might get hitched Texas style." Though he spoke in a humorous fake drawl, his eyes were wary and his voice held a quiver. "Whataya say?"

She pulled his head down to hers, until they were nose to nose. "I say, yes! Yes! Yes!"

Jeremiah put his arm around her, and as they walked past a trash can, Bridget dropped her container of pills in it and never looked back.

Epilogue

Bridget awakened and wasn't sure of her surroundings, except that she was in a bed with her husband, on top of him, with him still inside her.

After opening one eye, she knew where she was. Home. On the ranch, back in Utah. She opened both eyes and stared at the clock. It was 7:00 a.m. Shouldn't she be out of bed doing something? No. She didn't have anything to do—not yet, anyway. Not so with Jeremiah, though. Shouldn't he be up tending to the cattle?

Taylor! Where was Taylor? Her daughter rarely slept this late. Why were *they* sleeping so late? she wondered again. That was when it hit her. They had gotten married again yesterday afternoon in Texas, at her parents' house. Following the wedding, they had flown here while Taylor and Jeremiah's aunt had remained in Texas as guests of her parents.

Suddenly Bridget wanted to laugh out loud. She had never felt such happiness. Jeremiah had met her at the airport to ask her if she wanted to get hitched Texan style and she'd said a resounding yes, and they had gone on to do just that.

They had gone straight to her parents' house, and though the Martins were stunned at their intentions, they had come around and joined in the excitement.

Taylor and Jeremiah's aunt had flown into town while hasty arrangements were made. Bridget's mother had been in charge, and she had loved every minute of it. With her careful planning, the ceremony had gone off without a snafu.

"Do you, Bridget Martin, take this man to be your lawfully wedded husband...?"

"I do."

Following that exchange of vows—vows that she remembered taking this time—the few guests had laughed and clapped.

At the reception, Tiffany, her maid of honor, had managed to get her alone.

"I still can't believe you, Bridget. You really did it this time."

Bridget giggled. "Isn't it wonderful? Isn't *he* wonderful?"

"I think I'm going to be sick."

Bridget slapped her friend on the shoulder. "You're awful. Just wait till you fall in love."

"Don't count on that happening. I'm immune to that stuff. Besides, I like me, myself and I too much."

"You're full of it, Tiff."

"Me? What about you? Good God, your dad even came around. You were set up in private practice here, with all the financial backing you'd ever need."

"Well, I can set up practice in Hurricane, as well."

Tiffany snorted. "What'll you defend? The neighbor's bull that gets through the fence?"

Jeremiah chose that moment to saunter over to his wife. "What are you two conspiring about?"

Before either one could answer him, Taylor interrupted, running up to Bridget, looking pristine in her pink flower-girl dress and hugging her. "I love you, Mommy."

"And I love you, too, sweetheart," Bridget said, then surrendered the child to Aunt Lilah, who took Taylor to have some cake.

Tiffany focused her attention back on Jeremiah and answered his question, her lips twitching. "We weren't conspiring. At least, I wasn't."

This time Jeremiah snorted, though with a grin. "I'll bet."

"Incidentally, you look great," Tiffany added, winking at Bridget.

Jeremiah was wearing black jeans, a black tail coat with a vest, a white tuxedo shirt and a bolo tie. A black Stetson completed his ensemble.

"You like my getup?" he asked.

"As much as I hate to admit it, I sure do."

A wicked smile crossed his face. "Too bad you're still hooked on the bright lights. If you came back with us, Tiff, I could probably round up a cowboy for you, especially if you put on some tight fittin' jeans."

"Yeah, right."

Bridget giggled. "That's a game of no chance! We'll never see this filly in the boonies again!"

Jeremiah laughed, then put his arm around his wife and pulled her close. "It's time we left this party. We've got ranch business to take care of."

"Monkey business, you mean," Tiffany said, all grins.

Jeremiah answered her grin, then kissed Bridget on the temple. "That, too, of course."

"Our flight leaves soon, Tiff. When will I see you again?" Bridget's tone was suddenly sad.

"The next time you come back to the bright lights, so you'd best give me enough hugs to last us."

"Okay, ladies, that's all of that sudsy stuff I can handle." Jeremiah picked Bridget up and carried her toward the house.

"Where do you think you're goin', Davis?" someone shouted from the crowd as a cheer went up.

"Gotta get out of these duds. My collar's about to choke me to death."

Inside, Bridget looked down at her husband, then slowly ran her hand over the front of his jeans, a mischievous smile on her face. "That's not all that's choking to death."

He kissed her long and hard. "If we didn't have a plane to catch, Mrs. Davis, I'd make you pay for that remark."

Later, he *did* make her pay. The instant they set foot in the ranch house, they dropped their luggage, ripped off their clothes and jumped into bed.

Now, as Bridget peered down at her sleeping husband, she propped her chin on her elbows and sighed, thinking she was the luckiest woman in the world.

"Mmm, what a nice way to wake up."

"Think so, huh?" she whispered, beginning to move. She felt him harden beneath her.

"Ah, that feels so good, but shouldn't we be up, dressed and checking out that place I found for your law office?" He sounded like he was strangling.

She increased the pace just a bit. "What's wrong with later?"

Jeremiah groaned. "Nothing, as long as we do it. I want you to continue with your career."

She stopped moving and stared into his eyes. "I want to, too, and I will, as long as it doesn't interfere with my wifely duties."

"Such as cooking and gardening, huh?"

Bridget giggled and started riding him harder. "Absolutely. You just wait, I'm going to make you the best damn rancher's wife in the county, if not the entire state."

"I love you more than you'll ever know," he said with a groan.

"And I love you."

"So how 'bout we stop talking and finish this monkey business *you* started?"

"I didn't think you'd ever ask."

He pulled her down to him, and only a loving silence filled the room.

* * * * *

SILHOUETTE® Desire®

COMING NEXT MONTH

It's Silhouette Desire's 1000th birthday! Join us for a spectacular three-month celebration, starring your favorite authors and the hottest heroes of the decade!

#997 BABY DREAMS—Raye Morgan

The Baby Shower
Sheriff Rafe Lonewolf couldn't believe his feisty new prisoner was the innocent woman she claimed to be. But a passionate night with Cami Bishop was suddenly making *him* feel criminal!

#998 THE UNWILLING BRIDE—Jennifer Greene

The Stanford Sisters
Paige Stanford's new neighbor was sexy, smart…and single! Little did she know Stefan Michaelovich wanted to make *her* his blushing bride!

#999 APACHE DREAM BRIDE—Joan Elliott Pickart

When Kathy Maxwell purchased a dream catcher, she had no idea she'd soon catch herself an Apache groom! But could her dream really come true…or would she have to give up the only man she ever loved?

#1000 MAN OF ICE—Diana Palmer

Silhouette Desire #1000!
After one tempestuous night with irresistible Barrie Bell, May's MAN OF THE MONTH, Dawson Rutherford, swore off love forever. Now the only way he could get the land he wanted was to make Barrie his temporary bride.

#1001 INSTANT HUSBAND—Judith McWilliams

The Wedding Night
Nick St. Hilarion needed a mother for his daughter, not a woman for himself to love! But when Ann Lennon arrived special delivery, he realized he might not be able to resist falling for his mail-order wife!

#1002 BABY BONUS—Amanda Kramer

Debut Author
Leigh Townsend was secretly crazy about sexy Nick Romano, but she wasn't going to push him to propose! So she didn't tell him he was going to be a daddy—or else he would insist on becoming a husband, too.

MILLION DOLLAR SWEEPSTAKES
AND EXTRA BONUS PRIZE DRAWING

No purchase necessary. To enter the sweepstakes, follow the directions published and complete and mail your Official Entry Form. If your Official Entry Form is missing, or you wish to obtain an additional one (limit: one Official Entry Form per request, one request per outer mailing envelope) send a separate, stamped, self-addressed #10 envelope (4 1/8" x 9 1/2") via first class mail to: Million Dollar Sweepstakes and Extra Bonus Prize Drawing Entry Form, P.O. Box 1867, Buffalo, NY 14269-1867. Request must be received no later than January 15, 1998. For eligibility into the sweepstakes, entries must be received no later than March 31, 1998. No liability is assumed for printing errors, lost, late, non-delivered or misdirected entries. Odds of winning are determined by the number of eligible entries distributed and received.

Sweepstakes open to residents of the U.S. (except Puerto Rico), Canada and Europe who are 18 years of age or older. All applicable laws and regulations apply. Sweepstakes offer void wherever prohibited by law. Values of all prizes are in U.S. currency. This sweepstakes is presented by Torstar Corp., its subsidiaries and affiliates, in conjunction with book, merchandise and/or product offerings. For a copy of the Official Rules governing this sweepstakes, send a self-addressed, stamped envelope (WA residents need not affix return postage) to: MILLION DOLLAR SWEEP-STAKES AND EXTRA BONUS PRIZE DRAWING Rules, P.O. Box 4470, Blair, NE 68009-4470, USA.

SWP-ME96

SILHOUETTE®

Desire®

CELEBRATION 1000

A treasured piece of romance could be yours!

During April, May and June as part of
Desire's Celebration 1000 you can enter to win an
original piece of art used on an actual Desire cover!

Or you could win one of 300 autographed Man of the
Month books!

See Official Sweepstakes Rules for more details.

To enter, complete an Official Entry Form or a 3"x5" card by hand printing
"Silhouette Desire Celebration 1000 Sweepstakes", your name and address, and
mail to: **In the U.S.:** Silhouette Desire Celebration 1000 Sweepstakes, P.O. Box
9069, Buffalo, N.Y. 14269-9069, or **in Canada:** Silhouette Desire Celebration 1000
Sweepstakes, P.O. Box 637, Fort Erie, Ontario L2A 5X3. Limit one entry per
envelope. Entries must be sent via first-class mail and be received no later than
6/30/96. No liability is assumed for lost, late or misdirected mail.

**Official Entry Form—Silhouette Desire Celebration 1000
Sweepstakes**

Name: _____

Address: _____

City: _____

State/Province: _____

Zip or Postal Code: _____

Favorite Desire Author: _____

Favorite Desire Book: _____

SWEEPS

SILHOUETTE DESIRE® "CELEBRATION 1000" SWEEPSTAKES
OFFICIAL RULES—NO PURCHASE NECESSARY

To enter, complete an Official Entry Form or a 3"x5" card by hand printing "Silhouette Desire Celebration 1000 Sweepstakes," your name and address, and mail it to: In the U.S.: Silhouette Desire Celebration 1000 Sweepstakes, P.O. Box 9069, Buffalo, NY 14269-9069, or In Canada: Silhouette Desire Celebration 1000 Sweepstakes, P.O. Box 637, Fort Erie, Ontario L2A 5X3. Limit one entry per envelope. Entries must be sent via first-class mail and be received no later than 6/30/96. No liability is assumed for lost, late or misdirected mail.

Prizes: Grand Prize—an original painting (approximate value $1500 U.S.);300 Runner-up Prizes—an autographed Silhouette Desire® Book (approximate value $3.50 U.S./$3.99 CAN. each). Winners will be selected in a random drawing (to be conducted no later than 9/30/96) from among all eligible entries received by D.L. Blair, Inc., an independent judging organization whose decision is final.

Sweepstakes offer is open only to residents of the U.S. (except Puerto Rico) and Canada who are 18 years of age or older, except employees and immediate family members of Harlequin Enterprises Ltd., their affiliates, subsidiaries, and all agencies, entities and persons connected with the use, marketing or conduct of this sweepstakes. All federal, state, provincial, municipal and local laws apply. Offer void where prohibited by law. Taxes and/or duties are the sole responsibility of the winners. Any litigation within the province of Quebec respecting the conduct and awarding of prizes may be submitted to the Regie des alcools des courses et des jeux. All prizes will be awarded; winners will be notified by mail. No substitution for prizes is permitted. Odds of winning are dependent upon the number of eligible entries received.

Grand Prize winner must sign and return an Affidavit of Eligibility within 30 days of notification. In the event of noncompliance within this time period, prize may be awarded to an alternate winner. Any prize or prize notification returned as undeliverable may result in the awarding of that prize to an alternate winner. By acceptance of their prize, winners consent to the use of their names, photographs or likenesses for purposes of advertising, trade and promotion on behalf of Harlequin Enterprises Ltd., without further compensation unless prohibited by law. In order to win a prize, residents of Canada will be required to correctly answer a time-limited arithmetical skill-testing question administered by mail.

For a list of winners (available after October 31, 1996) send a separate self-addressed stamped envelope to: Silhouette Desire Celebration 1000 Sweepstakes Winners, P.O. Box 4200, Blair, NE 68009-4200.

SWEEPR

BEGINNING IN APRIL
FROM

SILHOUETTE®

Desire®

The Wedding Night

Three passion-filled stories about what happens when the wedding ring goes on...and the lights go out!

In April—A kidnapped bride is returned to her husband in
FORGOTTEN VOWS by Modean Moon

In May—A marriage of convenience turns into so much more in
INSTANT HUSBAND by Judith McWilliams

In June—A once-reluctant groom discovers he's a father in
THE PRODIGAL GROOM by Karen Leabo

THE WEDDING NIGHT: The excitement began when they said, "I do."

As seen on TV!
Free Gift Offer

With a Free Gift proof-of-purchase from any Silhouette® book,
you can receive a beautiful cubic zirconia pendant.

This gorgeous marquise-shaped stone is a genuine cubic
zirconia—accented by an 18" gold tone necklace.

(Approximate retail value $19.95)

Send for yours today...

compliments of ▼ *Silhouette*®
TM

To receive your free gift, a cubic zirconia pendant, send us one original proof-of-purchase, photocopies not accepted, from the back of any Silhouette Romance™, Silhouette Desire®, Silhouette Special Edition®, Silhouette Intimate Moments® or Silhouette Shadows™ title available in February, March or April at your favorite retail outlet, together with the Free Gift Certificate, plus a check or money order for $1.75 U.S./$2.25 CAN. (do not send cash) to cover postage and handling, payable to Silhouette Free Gift Offer. We will send you the specified gift. Allow 6 to 8 weeks for delivery. Offer good until April 30, 1996 or while quantities last. Offer valid in the U.S. and Canada only.

Free Gift Certificate

Name: _____

Address: _____

City: _____ State/Province: _____ Zip/Postal Code: _____

Mail this certificate, one proof-of-purchase and a check or money order for postage and handling to: SILHOUETTE FREE GIFT OFFER 1996. In the U.S.: 3010 Walden Avenue, P.O. Box 9057, Buffalo NY 14269-9057. In Canada: P.O. Box 622, Fort Erie,

---

FREE GIFT OFFER   079-KBZ-R

ONE PROOF-OF-PURCHASE

To collect your fabulous FREE GIFT, a cubic zirconia pendant, you must include this original proof-of-purchase for each gift with the properly completed Free Gift Certificate.

079-KBZ-R

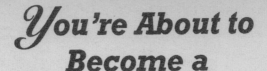